To Aua...

Paula.

nutters

P.J. DAVY

snowbooks

Proudly Published by Snowbooks in 2009

Snowbooks Ltd.
120 Pentonville Road
London
N1 9JN
Tel: 0207 837 6482
Fax: 0207 837 6348
email: info@snowbooks.com
www.snowbooks.com

British Library Cataloguing in Publication Data
A catalogue record for this book is available from the British Library.

ISBN 978-1-906727-21-5
Printed & bound by J F Print Ltd., Sparkford Somerset

For my father, David Brackston,
who is largely to blame for my sense of humour.

A Word from the Author

Huge thanks to Snowbooks for being brave enough to publish Nutters – mental health is not a naturally commercial subject, and being combined with comedy must make it a hard book to place in bookshops. Is it a comic novel? Is it a piece of general fiction? All I can say to help is that it is a story that seemed to want to be told in this way. Could we, perhaps, have a new shelf for tragi-comic novels?

I was asked by someone who read a proof copy if I was worried about making fun of 'them'. I was bemused. It had never occurred to me that there was a 'them'. My own, ten-year-long struggle with depression is where the idea for the story was formed. I recently lost a very dear cousin, Jonathan, who had lived all his adult life with manic depression, being sectioned thirty-three times. Other people close to me have also fought their own battles with mental health problems of one kind or another – some emerged triumphant, others did not emerge at all. So, as I see it, there is no 'them', only 'us'. Who can deny the madness of being in love, or the mind-warping power of grief? We all tread the perilously narrow path of sanity, tip-toed, arms akimbo. When we topple into the realms of lunacy, be it briefly or permanently, it helps if people do not avert their gaze but reach out a helping hand. Hence this book.

'But I don't want to go among mad people,' Alice remarked.
'Oh, you can't help that,' said the Cat. 'We're all mad here.
I'm mad. You're mad.'
'How do you know I'm mad?' said Alice.
'You must be,' said the Cat, 'or you wouldn't have come
here.'

Alice's Adventures in Wonderland – Lewis Carroll

CHAPTER ONE

The cell door slammed shut and Rufus was left listening to the dwindling footsteps of the custody sergeant. He had had better days, though at that moment it was hard to recall any of them with clarity. His left eye throbbed and his top lip oozed blood. He sat on the bench, then quickly stood up again. The smell of piss was stronger nearer the floor. Beer-filled piss. The orange mess in the corner of the room added high notes of vomit to the stench. He began to pace, three strides to the door, three back to the far wall. Every prison movie he had ever seen crowded into his head. He imagined spending weeks, months, years in such a place. Imagined himself ageing, pale and whiskery, his body disintegrating from malnutrition and lack of sunlight, his mind free-falling into madness. He reminded himself he was already officially mad, so that would save time. He attempted to pull himself together, something his mother had been urging him to do since he was twelve. Since the death of his father. Since his first episode.

He ran his hands through his hair and winced. Examination of his knuckles revealed more swelling and bruising. For a moment he was distracted by the thought that a fist connecting with a nose could come off the worse for the encounter. But then, it had been quite some nose. Short, broad, no doubt flattened by innumerable other fists slung in its direction over years. And the face it graced had clearly been constructed entirely of wood. Or possibly concrete.

Rufus sat down again, breathing only through his mouth in an effort to avoid the stink. After a few moments he began to taste the regurgitated Chicken Tikka Masala. He shut his mouth and his eyes, leaning back against the wall, trying to convince himself that it had all been worth it, and that he would do the same thing again without a moment's hesitation.

'Bollocks,' he said aloud, startled by the flat echo of his own voice. He glanced at the space where his watch had been. Why had they taken it? Did they think he was going to fashion some sort of lock-picking tool from its workings? Or a weapon, perhaps? Or did they fear he might try to choke himself with it? Why didn't they want him to know what the time was? How long were they planning to keep him there? Again, visions swam before his puffy eyes. *Papillon. The Count of Monte Cristo*. Morgan Freeman in dungarees. Oh God, were they going to make him wear dungarees?

After what seemed like several days but was in fact a little over an hour, Rufus heard voices at the far end of the corridor. One was a low murmur, the placatory tones of the heard-it-all-before copper. The other was louder, harsher: consonants sharpened into points, rounded vowels speaking of privilege and education, the unmistakeable cadence of confidence and authority. Unmissably a woman. A powerful, do-as-I-tell-you woman. Rufus hurried across the cell and put his ear to the cold metal of the door. The familiar voice was gathering understated force.

'I am his solicitor, Lydia Barnes.'

'Not the duty solicitor,' the officer remained unconvinced. 'Duty solicitor's Mr Adams tonight.'

'That is Mr Adams' bad fortune. I did not say I was the duty solicitor; I said I was here to see my client, and that is what I intend on doing.'

'Sorry, ma'am, there's no one to take you down to the cells right now. Why don't you come back in the morning?'

There was a brief, crackling pause. Lydia Barnes had had enough.

'Sergeant, I have not risen from my bed and driven across town at this uncivilised hour to be sent home again simply because your superiors see fit to under-staff this station. My client has a right to counsel, and counsel he shall have. What is more, I firmly believe that he is being held here on spurious charges and suggest that you refer me to your superior officer so that we can effect his immediate release.' Her voice took on a menacing softness, 'Or would you prefer me to return after breakfast with a suit for false imprisonment and breach of human rights, naming your good self as the responsible officer?'

Stilettos stabbed along the hallway. Rufus stepped back, tension stiffening his neck. Locks were undone. The door swung open. Lydia Barnes looked every day of her sixty-two years. No amount of elegant tailoring, relentlessly coiffured hair, or tastefully manicured fingernails could soften the woman. She appeared to be exactly what she was: successful, powerful, and untouchable. She had done an exceptionally good job over the years of distancing herself from the unfragrant masses that constituted her clients, her colleagues, and indeed her own family, and now that separateness had become irreversible. She regarded Rufus with wordless distaste. Rufus risked a rueful smile.

'Hello, Mummy,' he said.

Once outside the police station and in the sanctuary of Lydia's Bentley, he began to feel a little better. It was a still, clear night. As the car glided across the ancient stone bridge Rufus peered down at the silky water below. The moon reflected on its dark surface. A darting moorhen set up a series of tiny ripples, briefly distorting the image. The car sped on, leaving the centre of Hereford and turning left along the riverbank. Rufus was relieved to find his mother was taking him to his flat and not insisting he return with her to her own house. He had never felt comfortable in the place she still referred to as his home, even though her relief at his moving out eight years ago had been poorly masked. He knew he did not fit in at Ranelagh Road, with its graceful Georgian villas set discreetly back from the road, shielded by high walls, Laburnum, Privet, and Willow. In fact, the city itself seemed to him completely at odds with his own reality. Smart red brick town houses, quaint black and white buildings of ancient provenance, sparkling modern eateries and shopping arcades – it all spoke of safety, and steadiness, and order, and genteel restraint, and straightforward middle England. Sober, respectable, predictable. Everything Rufus was not, in fact. He dabbed at his lip with his mother's handkerchief.

'You look frightful,' she told him.

'You should see the other guy,' he winced, then dabbed some more. 'It was worth it,' he added, as much to himself as to her.

'A little contrition might be more appropriate.'

'I am not going to apologise for doing something I should have done sodding years ago. I am not taking any more crap.'

Lydia braked sharply at a set of lights and fixed Rufus with a glare. 'I don't think I know you at all any more. Brawling in a public house. Getting yourself arrested. And being proud of it.' The lights changed, and she urged the Bentley forward. 'Your father would have been heartbroken.'

'Let's thank God he's dead, then.' The moment the words were out, Rufus regretted them. There was something about his mother that made him say the wrong thing. Every time. No wonder she hated him. They travelled the remainder of the short journey in silence until Lydia stopped the car outside the converted warehouse that was now a small block of flats. She switched off the engine. Rufus made a feeble attempt at lifting the tension.

'Comin' up for coffee then, eh, darlin'?' he asked with overdone coarseness.

His mother did not look at him when she spoke. 'Rufus, when did you last see Dr Spinks?'

'Sod Dr Spinks – I'm tired of him. I'm tired of all of it. Don't worry, I'm taking my medication. And no, I don't feel suicidal, thanks for asking.' He climbed out of the car. 'In fact, I've never felt better.' He paused, leaning in through the open passenger door. He knew he should try harder, should find a way to tell her, to explain. But he could not. 'Thanks for coming,' he said at last, slipping into an exaggerated Hicksville American accent. 'Thanks for springing me from the County Jail!'

Lydia looked at him now. 'Just for once in your life try and take something seriously, Rufus.'

He watched her drive away, mulling over the ridiculousness of this instruction, given that his main problem was taking things with deathly seriousness too much of the time, and then hurried up the wrought-iron staircase and along the gangway that led to his front door. It was past two now, and the inhabitants of the other flats were silent, their windows dark. Rufus fumbled with his key in the lock, his knuckles smarting as they rubbed against the polished wood. As always, he felt immense relief at shutting the door on the rest of the world. He leaned against it for a moment, as if afraid someone might try to follow him in, might try to force their unwelcome way into the only place he ever felt remotely safe. He flicked the light switch and gazed about him. The open-plan space, bare floorboards, exposed brickwork, and chunky iron joists and pillars had been artfully put together, no doubt anticipating trendy young professionals. But Rufus had never had any truck with trendy, was not and never would be a professional anything, and was finding it harder and harder to live up to young. His thirty-fifth birthday of the previous year had been a shock. At least now he did not have to pretend to be hip or happening. Anyway, it was his flat; why shouldn't he furnish it exactly as he pleased? He liked the cracked and sagging brown leather sofa. He enjoyed the feel of the rag rug tickling his bare toes of a morning. He still got pleasure from his Rothko prints. The aged dentist's chair was perfect for reclining in when he needed to listen to Albinoni's *Adagio in G.* The stuffed red squirrel under its glass dome with its permanently startled expression often made him smile, even on bad days. What was it Kate called the whole effect? Shabby chic. That was it. Shabby chic. Or was it just shabby? It mattered not. Of course, she hated the squirrel. Said it offended on so many levels. It was, according to Kate, politically incorrect to the point of being incendiary; cruel and probably illegal, given the scarcity of the wretched creatures; unavoidably creepy; and just plain nasty. Well, she was entitled to her opinion. There had been a moment in their relationship once, briefly, when it looked like she might have moved in. The squirrel had been an issue then. A furry little bone or two of contention. But the madness had passed, the relationship faltered, and she and he had settled on being friends. Most people might have viewed this outcome as a failure of sorts. Rufus saw it as one of the few good and sensible things in his life. He had been rubbish at being Kate's boyfriend. They had been together for all the wrong reasons. Friends was better.

Rufus took a breath and tried to focus. There was work to be done. The events of the night had brought him to a decision, and that decision required action. He strode over to the kitchen area and tugged a black bin bag from the cupboard beneath the sink. He licked his fingers and struggled to open the rustling sack before sliding out the drawer to his left. He regarded the contents with narrowed eyes. In front of him was an impressive array of medication. There were small brown glass bottles of pills; large green bottles of pills; rectangular boxes of tablets and capsules; silver blister packs of lozenge-shaped medicaments; jars of herbal remedies; plastic tubs of doses of natural tranquillisers and equally natural stimulants. There were sticky bottles of stomach calming liquids to cancel out the side effects of the stronger prescription drugs. There were packets of chewy chalkiness claiming to do the same, and rattling jars of this and that, all declaring themselves to offer relief from something or other. Something or other he most likely would not have been suffering from had he not started with the pills in the small brown bottles. Or the large green bottles. Or the blister packs. Rufus picked up the nearest slender box. It felt familiar in his hand. He could tell just by the weight of it to the nearest tablet how many were left. He stroked the label with his thumb. His name was printed above the date of prescription, along with instructions to take two tablets morning and night, and a warning of the dangers of either exceeding or decreasing the dosage without first consulting a GP.

'Sod it!' said Rufus, feeling a steely determination grip him. He dropped the box into the bin bag and then selected a glass bottle of green and yellow capsules. He hesitated for a fraction of a moment before consigning it to the bag. He grabbed a handful of packets and repeat prescription leaflets and stuffed them in. Next he yanked the drawer from its runners and upended it, sending the contents cascading into their plastic oblivion with a satisfying rattling and pinging, like an enthusiastically shaken rain stick. Rufus hurried into the bathroom and pulled open the glass cabinet. Standing to one side, he used his arm to scoop the entire contents into the bin bag. Nothing was spared. His bedside locker received the same purge, as did his desk, his jacket pockets, his spongebag, even the dusty First Aid box that had lain waiting for him to buy a car for nearly three years. At last, the deed done, he deposited the bag outside his front door, double locked the same against second thoughts, and flopped onto his unmade bed. As drowsiness began to blur his vision, his gaze settled on the silver-framed photo on the mantelpiece across the room. The picture showed him as a boy of eleven, proudly sporting the uniform of his prep-school, while beside him, plumper, five crucial years older, wearing the blazer of a sixth-former, his brother Matthew beamed. Rufus let his eyes close, the snapshot of himself and his sibling fading as sleep took him, only to be replaced by an image from a year later. Both boys stood close once again, but this time the school uniforms were swapped for dark suits, and the grins exchanged for sombre expressions. They were standing at their father's graveside in the final moments of his funeral service. Lydia stood beside them, dry-eyed and dignified. The vicar intoned:

'...in sure and certain hope of the resurrection...'

Twelve-year-old Rufus began to breathe rapidly. His hand went to his throat as the air rushing in and out of his lungs seemed to supply no oxygen.

'...ashes to ashes...'

In seconds Rufus had begun to gasp noisily. His brother turned to him, concerned.

'Rufus? Rufus, are you all right?'

Rufus was not all right. Indeed, at that moment Rufus knew with chilling certainty that he would probably never be all right ever again. He sank to his knees, wheezing, struggling for breath as the panic attack tightened its grip on him. Lydia gave her son a look blacker than the exquisitely cut wool suit she was wearing.

'Rufus!' she hissed. 'Pull yourself together!'

Matthew knelt beside his brother, sliding a protective but useless arm around his shoulders. Embarrassed mourners fidgeted. The vicar hesitated, but a savage nod from Lydia forced him to continue. Rufus was unable to breathe, swallow, or speak, so that it was with enormous relief that he eventually slumped sideways onto the damp grass and passed out.

CHAPTER TWO

Rufus woke up as he so often did, sitting bolt upright, mouth wide, arms flailing, gasping for air, jolted awake by some poorly wired synapse that warned of imminent death if he did not either fight or flee. As the room swam into focus, the pain of his freshly re-opened split lip roused him from his state of terror. He was in bed. He was at home. He was safe. There was nothing to fight. There was nothing from which to flee. Except himself. He closed his eyes and took three steady, slow breaths. He dug his nails into his palms and focused on the sensation. The stinging of his lip, however, was a more effective distraction. He sat very still, quelling the urge to run outside, waiting for his adrenalin levels to subside sufficiently for him to risk moving. As always, the manner in which his brain and body seemed to work with each other but against what he knew to be real and sound and good for him irritated him intensely. Maddened him, even. If he could only harness all that energy, all that effort, all that certainty of impending doom, and train it to be helpful instead of self-destructive, life might actually be worth living. But he could not. His sub-conscious and his primitive self were convinced death lurked around every corner and that it was their job to alert him to this constant peril. The fact that this supposed technique for evading sabre-toothed tigers or parrying blows from perpetually raised clubs had on more than one occasion driven Rufus to try to take his own life seemed to him to be the height of absurdity. But then, as Dr Spinks had delighted in telling him, the sub-conscious has no sense of irony. It would not get the joke. Another reason to despise it, as far as Rufus could see. It was bad enough being possessed by some cruel demon who gained pleasure only from torturing its host. It was salt in the wound that the damn thing didn't even have a sense of humour.

Rufus risked opening his eyes to check the time. Nine-thirty. Nine-thirty!

'Shit!'

He clambered off the bed and hurried into the bathroom. The broad mirror on the far wall did nothing to make him feel better. His clothes looked as if he had slept in them because he had. His left eye now resembled a psychedelic Easter egg. It ached dully. His bruised and bloody lip gave him a ridiculous trout pout. He badly needed a shave, and his shaggy blonde hair had crossed some vital line between casually dishevelled and sad mess. He splashed his face with cold water, strode through the flat, checking his pocket for his keys before going out, stumbling over the bin bag of medication on the gangway.

The day clearly had no interest in his fragile state and boasted a sun so bright Rufus could only proceed by squinting myopically. Scrunching up his wounded eye caused it to throb once more. He wished he had taken the time to ferret in the fridge for orange juice; his throat felt gritty and tight. Head down, he hurried along the riverbank to the ornate iron footbridge, barely noticing how pretty the park looked, or how sparkling the water in the morning sunlight, or how quaint the mallards and coots it bore silently south. He scrunched along the gravel path that led through the old castle ruins, past the inappropriately bright beds of tulips, alongside the lovingly tended lawns of the green until he reached the Cathedral Square itself. Ordinarily, when he had time to notice, he enjoyed sneering at the tweeness and self-conscious loveliness of the collection of town houses that formed three sides of the square. Today he was late, late, late. Late for Kate. And she would chide him for it, and tell him he had more free time than anyone she knew, apart from her grandparents, and they were retired, so they didn't count. She would remind him that his was a life of leisure, that no one relied upon him for anything, and that he was rarely required to be anywhere or do anything. So, her theory ran, on the few occasions when he was actually supposed to be somewhere, doing something, it was doubly insulting if he could not be bothered to turn up on time. As he pulled open the door of the cathedral, celestial voices greeted him. He made his way quickly along the west wall, trying hard to be inconspicuous, his leather soles slapping unhelpfully against the stone flags. The choir had clearly finished warming up and was now rehearsing full throttle, chins up, eyes bright, their music soaring into the beautiful ceiling from where it spread out and fell in a spring shower of soft, mellifluous notes. Rufus nudged his way into place among the tenors. He tired to focus on the energetic little director of the choir and to pick up the piece, but his voice was thin and cold and he was acutely aware of his lateness and his alarming appearance. Kate leant out of the soprano section to stare at him. She gave him a stern frown, her pretty, dark features rearranging themselves into clear disapproval, quickly followed by raised brows of enquiry. Rufus attempted to stick his tongue out at her then wished he hadn't. He redoubled his efforts to enter into the music. Mozart's Requiem was an old favourite of his, though the choral snob in him inwardly winced at the less than perfect rendition the Belmont Choir was currently managing. It wasn't that they were a poor choir. Quite the opposite, in fact. Their concerts were sell-outs and there had even been talk of cutting a CD. But Rufus had his favourite recording of the piece and nothing could live up to that, however heartfelt, however fresh, however personal. For him the apotheosis of musical endeavour, the finest possible example of Herr Mozart's work, was to be found only via the throats of the Christ College Choir as conducted by Heinrich Westbaum and recorded at St Martin's-in-the-Field in 1997. He had the CD. He had the thing on his iPod. He knew every nuance, every trill, every minuscule pause which made that recording The One. He would have been happier singing something a little less…well, just something a little less. At least they were only attempting the first movement. This was to be the opening number for their Summer Concert at the cathedral. It was a popular choice. For himself, Rufus would enjoy more Kate's solo performance. The piece had yet to be decided upon, but he knew she would be magnificent. She always was. Even when she was not well she remained able to sing. Hers was a voice of such clarity, such sweetness, such contained power it moved many to tears. Rufus was one of that multitude. Sometimes, when Kate was being particularly infuriating, or when she had altered into that other Kate whom no one could reach, Rufus would remind himself of the beauty of her voice. It helped him. It reminded him of what was possible. Of what a good day looked like.

He quickly realised that his vocal chords were too tired, too parched, and too feeble to produce any sound worth hearing and resorted to miming with a studious expression on his face. He avoided looking at Kate until the rehearsal was over.

'Remember, tomorrow evening at six-thirty,' the conductor, Philip, tried to make himself heard above the murmuring and rustling of sheet music, 'please can everyone make a supreme effort to be on time. There's a lot to get through. Thank you, everybody.'

As the singers melted away Rufus was left standing in front of Kate, who was examining his face with a mixture of pity and disgust.

'Well?' she put her head on one side, her chocolate brown curls springing free of their inexpertly applied scrunchie and falling about her face as she did so. 'Are you going to tell me how you got like that, or are we going to play Twenty Questions?' Her Yorkshire accent, completely absent in her singing voice, now reasserted itself firmly. 'You look chuffing awful, by the way,' she added.

'Thank you so much for those kind words,' Rufus stepped past her. 'Come on, I'll tell all over brunch.'

She fell into step beside him, her energetic pacing an easy match for his long stride, her restlessness making up for their considerable difference in leg length.

'You're buying the Danish, then,' she told him. 'If I've to listen to some sordid tale of what you get up to on a Friday night, I'll need a quality sugar hit.'

'Luigi's then?'

'Bloody right, Luigi's.'

They made their way across the velvety green, down Broad Street, and entered the modern riverside development that housed their café of choice. Despite its name there was nothing noticeably Italian about the place. It was on the fourth floor of a building too small to be called a mall or arcade, but too fragmented to be a department store. Aside from the pastries, the finest feature of the place was the panoramic window that made up one wall, giving a dizzying view of the river below. The polished wooden floor, chrome fittings, and glass tables meant that even on quiet days the room clattered and chinged and squeaked and rattled, every tiny sound or movement echoing and reverberating around the space. Rufus and Kate slid their trays along the shiny silver rails. Rufus selected an apple Danish, Kate insisted on her favourite apricot custard version. She tutted at Rufus as he ordered Regular coffees so that he was persuaded to change his order to Grand. The girl on the till gave him a funny look, taking in his battered face. He risked a smile, causing his lip to start oozing blood once more. The girl quickly looked away again.

'Why "Grand"?' he asked Kate as they threaded their way between tables to the window. 'That's not Italian. And the pastries are Danish anyway. Danish made in Hereford, that is. Why can't it just be Large? I'll have a Large Coffee, please. Sounds much better to me.'

'Sit yourself down, stop your blathering, and tell me how come you look like you got hired to go three rounds with a kangaroo.' She tucked into her pastry.

Rufus tipped brown sugar into his latte, enjoying the moment of it sinking through the froth. 'Last night I had an epiphany,' he said.

'That what you call it? Looks more like a punch in the face to me.'

'I was in that pub on the other side of the market.'

'The Soldier's Arms? That's rough as a badger's bum. What were you doing in there?'

'I'd been walking. Thinking. I was passing. It's not important. The point is there was this thug in there. You know the type: no neck, hair, or intellect. Not very high up on the food chain...'

'My God, you're such a snob.'

'...always anchorman on tug-of-war teams. Anyway, he must have seen that piece in the paper about the Belmont Hospital Choir,' he stirred his coffee vigorously.

'The one with the photo? Good of me, I thought. You looked like a serial killer.'

'He recognized me. Started making nasty little comments. Went on about nutters, care in the community, where was my minder...'

'Usual chuffing rubbish then.'

'*Exactly!* Same thing, *again.* There I am having a quiet drink and this imbecile with the time-shared brain cell is questioning *my* fitness for society. That's when I decided, *No more!* I wasn't having it.' To emphasise his point Rufus began to bang his spoon on the table, underlining each determined word. 'I went over and told him so. Said he could keep his facile remarks to himself or suffer the consequences.'

'And that's when he hit you?' Kate gently took the spoon from his hand.

'No. The bastard laughed at me!' Rufus's breathing had become ragged and irregular, his pupils dilated. 'What right had he to laugh at me, for Christsake? So I hit him. Wham! Right on his fat little nose. I've had enough with being labelled a nutter, I'm telling you. I choose sanity.'

'Picking a fight with a man twice your size? Oh aye, very sane.'

By now Rufus was hyperventilating, his whole body moving to the speedy rhythm of air rasping in and out of his lungs with unnecessary force.

Kate frowned at him and then turned to the table next to their own. Two middle-aged women, well-dressed and elegantly made up, sat quietly with cups of Earl Grey. By the expressions on their faces, it was clear Rufus's agitated state had not escaped their notice.

'Excuse me, ladies,' Kate smiled at them, 'would y'mind?' She indicated the paper bag that lay on the table in front of them. Without waiting for a response she gently shook the contents (a paisley printed notebook) from the bag. 'Won't be a mo',' she told them. She handed the bag to Rufus who snatched it wordlessly and held it to his mouth. He breathed into it deeply, the brown paper flapping in and out like a balloon rapidly inflating and deflating again.

Kate took a swig of her coffee and wiped foam from her top lip. 'Look,' she said, 'we all feel like that from time to time, Rufus. It's in every nutter's job description. It can get to you. I should know. That doesn't mean it's a good idea to go around thumping apes, now does it?'

Rufus struggled to respond through the bag. 'I've made my decision. I refuse to be seen as a lunatic first and a human being second any longer. I've already binned all my medication.'

'Oooh, risky move, that.'

'And I'm going to see the ridiculous, over-paid, patronising Dr Spinks and sack him this very afternoon.'

'Now you know I've had the hots for your psychiatrist for years. Don't expect me to take agin just because you have.'

'Thank you for your loyalty. Anyway, I knew you'd think I was…'

'Mad?'

Rufus closed his eyes for a moment and concentrated on regaining control of his breathing. Once he was sure it had returned to as near normal as it was going to get, he passed the bag back to Kate. She watched him for a few seconds, then turned to their fellow diners with the brightest of smiles.

'Ta very much,' she said.

The women recoiled from the paper bag as it flopped damply on the table in front of them. Rufus and Kate finished their pastries in silence.

At last, when Kate had noisily drained her Cappuccino, she tried to reason with him. 'You've got to be realistic. If you want to cut down on your medication do it properly. Talk to the gorgeous Dr Spinks first.'

'No. You're missing the point. I'm not playing that game any more.'

'It's your sanity,' Kate said with a shrug, 'who am I to tell you how to hang on to it? But I will be the first to say "I told you so" when it all goes tits up. Which it will.' She stood up, her chair scraping against the stylish floor. 'Come on. Some of us have demeaning part-time jobs to go to.'

Outside the day continued to be relentlessly cheerful. They walked the short distance back up Broad Street, through the narrow alley beside St Mary's, and down West Street to the Quickshopper supermarket. Rufus already felt drained. Simply trying to explain to Kate what he was going to do had brought on another panic attack. It was not the promising start to the New Improved Rufus Waters he had been hoping for.

'Well, this is me,' said Kate at the entrance to the shop.

'Go on, then,' Rufus found it hard to look at her. He was trying to keep the nervous edge out of his voice, but he knew she knew him too well. 'Go and slave your life away, Little Dorrit.'

'We don't all have fat juicy trust funds to keep us warm. Anyway, I like my job.'

'Of course you do, all that stimulating variety and limitless challenge. Which shelves are you stacking today? I think condiments and pickles would be my favourite. One can never have too many pickled onions, in my opinion.'

'You're just jealous 'cos nobody'd trust you with a pickled onion.'

A shout from further up the street interrupted their fond farewell. Rufus turned to see Teach approaching. In the unforgiving brightness he looked even more cadaverous than usual. Like Rufus he was tall and lean, but somehow Teach had drifted beyond slender into skeletal. He had never revealed his true age to his friends, though Rufus, going on details of his life exploits, had him at about fifty. His body, however, looked a good decade older. Here was a man who had grasped with both bony hands every mind-altering drug available for many years, and every chemically assisted adventure was mapped out on his pallid face. There was still a gleam in his eye, a zest for living that was most likely what had got him into so much trouble in the first place. His mind must have, in his youth, been astoundingly sharp. As a classics teacher at the Whitecross Boys' School he had been loved, respected, revered even. Now, though the intellect still sparked, somewhere in the unfathomable muddle that was Teach's brain, vital connections were no longer being made. Fragments of Latin and snippets of the profound thoughts of the Ancients bobbed to the surface like so much cerebral flotsam and jetsam, but the crucial applications of context, clarity, and indeed meaning seemed to have sunk without trace. As ever, Teach was clutching bulging carrier bags, each stuffed to bursting with things gleaned from the street. It was, Rufus had long ago decided, as if by gathering rubbish and making sense of it Teach somehow felt he was making sense of his own chaotic existence. Of himself, perhaps.

Teach raised a hand, and therefore a bag, in salute, 'Good morning, friends. How are we this bright and shiny new day? My word, Ruf, look at your face!'

Kate gave him a quick kiss. Rufus was surprised at the little twinge of jealousy he always felt when she did this. He knew it was a friendly kiss, affectionate, caring, nothing remotely flirtatious or sexual. Still, she never gave him kisses like that. Since they had decided to be Friends she never kissed him in any way at all. Was he so unlovable? Or would it be blurring the edges, was that it? Was she worried she might lean in to peck a Friend and be overwhelmed by the desire to snog a Lover? He doubted it, somehow.

'I'm late for work,' she told Teach, 'and he's not nuts any more.'

'Really?' Teach seemed only mildly surprised.

Rufus waved her comment aside, 'She's taking the piss. Ignore her.'

'Well, isn't that what you just told me? He's decided to leave us to join the ranks of the normal. Doesn't want to be in our gang anymore. No more medication. No more therapy. Just a lovely, clean, straightforward normal life. Sounds chuffing dull to me.'

'I suppose you're going to tell me it won't work too.'

'Not at all, not at all,' Teach was quick to reassure him. 'I have every faith in you, Ruf. You're quite the sanest person I know.'

Kate laughed, 'Imagine!'

'No,' Teach went on, 'I truly believe if anyone could pull off such an audacious move it would be you, my friend. Go for it. *Carpe Tedium*, as they say. Oh, bye then, Kate.' He paused to watch her disappear through the automatic doors, and then held up his carrier bags to show Rufus. 'I've found some gems already this morning, Ruf. Some real treasures. Want to see?'

'For once, Teach, I'd be happy to.'

'Really?'

'Yup. Nothing is going to stop me feeling positive today. Not even the results of your street-combing. Come on, I'll buy you a pint.'

They began to walk through the ever-thickening Saturday crowds.

'Highly decent of you, Ruf. I think you'll be impressed this time,' he whipped out a glove from the top of the first plastic carrier. 'Look. Look at this. Hardly worn. And the craftsmanship. Beautifully worked leather.'

'Perfect, Teach, for all those one-handed people needing a glove.'

'Ahh, I thought about that. Golfers!'

Rufus glanced at the thing, 'Wrong hand,' he said.

'You don't say? Shame. Never played myself. Never had time while I was teaching, though the school is right next to the golf course.' He muttered on, digging deeper into the bags. Seconds later he gave a triumphant cry and pulled out a hideous piece of costume jewellery. 'There! Could any man deny the beauty in such a thing?'

Rufus glanced at it. 'I know one,' he muttered.

'Ah yes, maybe. I see. I know exactly what you're thinking – *simplex munditiis!*'

'Amazing! How do you do that?'

'"Elegance in simplicity" – or was it stupidity? Either is a valid view, I suppose…'

'Teach.'

'Yes?'

They had reached the heavy wooden doors of The Bunch of Grapes. Rufus paused with his hand against the brass plate.

'Alcohol first, Latin later, OK?'

'Oh absolutely,' he followed him inside. 'With you there, Ruf. Absolutely. What did you do to your face, by the way?'

CHAPTER THREE

Kate wasn't fibbing when she said she liked her job. It might not be everybody's idea of a good time, but it suited her needs. It was undemanding. It was unchallenging. It kept stress levels to a minimum and allowed her thoughts to travel to other more interesting places. She had been offered a job on the checkout but had turned it down. Checkout meant you had to talk to people. To smile at them. To pretend you gave a raggedy rat's arse about how their day was going. Kate shuddered at the idea of having her head filled with all that small talk and pointless blathering day after day. Here, on shelves, or more specifically on shelves on aisle seven known as Personal Hygiene and Grooming, she was left alone. Aside from the odd bleary-eyed shopper asking for directions to gripe water, or nervous men enquiring in lowered voices about haemorrhoid cream, nobody bothered her. She was free to get on with topping up toothpaste or filling gaps in deodorant without being forced to smile or speak.

In fact, there were only two things about her job she did not like. The first was the uniform. The nylon black trousers she could live with, but the spotted yellow tabard should have got someone somewhere shot. On her first day it had been presented to her with a care label (cool wash, do not iron, tumble dry at own risk) describing it as Polka Dot Wild Primrose. Kate had seen a few primroses in her time and none of them had the wince-making sharpness of the tabard. Demented Daffodil, she had decided. More suitable all round, really.

The second thing that made her grind her teeth was the Quickshopper Music Channel that played non-stop for every hour the shop was open. In her first week, the endless assault on her ears of Pop and Easy Listening had pushed her close to breaking point. What daft beggar had called it Easy Listening? How was that Easy? Lyrics about flaky men and faithless women all set to melodies composed in a musical range so narrow you'd think only two keys and one octave had ever been invented. The selection of hits (hits!) had been made by some scary computer programme that had decided shoppers spent more money if they had a diet of Kenny Rogers, Celine Dion, and Neil Diamond rammed down their throats. And what the chuff was a Cracklin' Rose, anyway? Once, Kate had smuggled in her iPod and worn plaits to try and hide the wires but the Manager, Mr Morgan, had spotted her conducting a lovely bit of Elgar with a tube of denture cleaning tablets, and that was the end of that. Eventually, knowing that she had to do something, Kate had developed a method of singing inside her head that successfully shut out the aural abuse. This had the added bonus of allowing her to practice whatever it was the choir was currently rehearsing. She had to be careful not to let her lips move. She knew she was always being watched for signs of strangeness. Mr Morgan saw her as a necessary challenge; that was obvious. She ticked a very important box in the Annual Human Resources Survey. He knew it, and she knew it. And he knew she knew it. He needed Kate, not to keep a keen hazel eye or two on the stocks of bubble bath, but to comply with company policy regarding the employment of anyone who might fit the description of having a Learning Disability. Chuffing wonderful. Here she was, top student of her final year at school, a singing scholarship to the Royal Academy, and the only reason she had this job was that her mental health record put her in there with the poor beggars who could barely write their names. Nowhere on Mr Morgan's form was there anything to suggest a difference between a person with learning difficulties and one suffering from bi-polar disorder. Feeble minded covered the lot.

Kate had just finished stacking sanitary towels as high as they would safely go (regardless of wings) when she noticed two familiar faces round the corner at the end of the aisle. She pretended not to see them as the women halted their trolleys at what they must have thought was a safe distance.

'I'm surprised she's still here,' the bottle blonde said in a whisper that could have been heard in Tinned Goods, 'after what happened last summer...'

'They can't sack them,' Edgy Bob in Smock Top explained. 'It's against discrimination.'

'Even so,' Bottle Blonde shook her head, 'it can't be good for business, can it? Letting someone... *like that*... work here.'

Kate slid sideways to Hair Removal and focused her attention on facial bleach. There was no point letting it get to her. Best keep your head down. The women cruised past, silent and scathing, their stares daring Kate to respond. She resisted the urge to roll her eyes wildly, let her tongue loll out, and rush at them drooling. They already thought she was barking. Why should she make their day by proving them right? And anyway, her attention was needed elsewhere; there was an empty space where bikini wax strips should be. Only her vigilance could prevent a scene of intimate hairy horror at the Leisure Centre.

Once the women had moved off, Kate allowed herself to relax a little. She didn't need reminding by them or any bugger else about last summer. Or the summer before that. Why was it always summer? She could hardly blame the heat, as every August she could remember since the family had moved to Hereford had been dull and disappointing. Cardigan weather, her mother called it. Cardigan weather in cardigan country. Kate experienced a violent pang of longing for London. She had only been there for one short year. An academic year. A year that ended in a summer, as so many of Kate's years did. Thinking back to her three terms at the Royal Academy of Music was always exquisitely painful. She knew the truth of it could not possibly be as wonderful, as glorious, as golden and shining as her memory of how it had been. But that didn't stop her holding those precious moments close. Moments of achievement, of hope, of promise, of possibility. Moments where she had been regarded differently. As a singer. No, sod it, not just a singer – a rare talent, a voice, a songbird just about to spread her wings and take to the world stage of classical music. She had been chuffing fantastic. And then... and then...

Mercifully, a lot of the worst bits were a blur. It was often like that. Everyone else could recall every little sordid incident of her madness, but to Kate it was a fuzzy mess, patchy, incomplete, and strangely distant. Just as well, really. It was bad enough having other people tell her about the awfulness of it all. She didn't want to relive it in her own head. Sometimes though, when she least expected it, flashes of those times, missing pieces of the lurid jigsaw, would pop up behind closed lids when she was falling asleep, or in front of her face when she was awake, even. She might be sitting on a bus and a scene would appear, as if Cresta Transport had suddenly decided to install in-flight entertainment in all their vehicles. And there she'd be, playing out some horrendous happening of a lost August afternoon. Chasing imaginary impala through Regent's Park. Embracing the guards at Buckingham Palace. Trying to wash the hair of an unconscious tramp with a bottle of Evian and some of her favourite shampoo. Screaming at a terrified West Indian girl, completely failing to get her to understand that she was the love child of Tony Blair and Whoopi Goldberg. Running naked through Brewer Street Market. Being dragged, handcuffed and raving, into a police car. These video-nasties could ambush her at any time, without warning. Mostly she had learnt to let them roll by, ignore them, shake them from her head, and press on. Sometimes they took her breath away. Only once did they make her cry.

It had always struck Kate as bizarre that she cried more when people were trying to help her than when she was just blundering about on her own, coping as best she could. She had wept rivers the first time she ended up in the Belmont. It wasn't the first time she had been sectioned, but it was when she lost her place at the Academy. It was when she'd had to face up to the fact that she was, basically, stuffed. She might have the voice of an angel, but she had the mind of a loon, and that mind would never allow her to have the glittering, sparkly, fabulous career she had, up till that point, always believed was hers for the taking. Accepting the truth of this had been hard. During that first stay at The Belmont, she now saw, she had experienced something close to grief for the life that had been so abruptly and brutally snuffed out before it had even had a chance to get going. She had been first numb with shock, then miserably sad, then angry. It was while she was busy with the angry bit that she'd met Rufus. She had been to enough of the group therapy sessions to know they did nothing for her, but Rufus was a first-timer. That day, when he had come shuffling into the room and slumped heavily onto a chair at the far side of the circle from herself, Kate experienced a fleeting moment of pity towards him. He looked so frail, so lost, so beaten. Her sympathy hadn't lasted. The second he opened his mouth she hated him. Even with medication slowing his speech and blurring the edges of his words he sounded arrogant. Posh and arrogant. Posh and rich and arrogant. Chuffing wanker. Kate had little time for privileged Mummy's boys with more money than was good for them who got a bit down when life didn't go the way they wanted it, and then went around telling everyone they were depressed and couldn't cope. Mental Health Lite.

'It's people like you,' she told him, 'give the rest of us a bad name.'

'Sorry?'

'You heard.'

'Now, Kate,' the Counsellor put in, 'this is Rufus's first time in the group. I think we should give him a chance to settle in, don't you?'

'Well, he makes me chuffing sick. Doesn't know the meaning of mental illness.'

'I do beg your pardon,' Rufus was not smiling. 'I hadn't realised this was a competition.'

'Oh aye,' Kate's accent thickened with her increasing anger, 'that'd be right. Smart arse. You sit there, fuzzy from a couple of Diazepam, like a teetotal vicar's wife who's been at the sherry. Chuffing lightweight. Depression my arse. What have you ever had to be depressed about?'

Other members of the group, smelling blood, began to murmur and jeer, egging Kate on and scowling at Rufus.

The counsellor held up a hand. 'We're not here to judge, Kate.'

'It's right, though, isn't it?' Kate struggled through the weight of Lithium to put force behind her words. 'He's had everything, all his life. Posh school, posh house, shed loads of money. Skiing every year, shouldn't bloody wonder. Doesn't even have to get a job.'

Rufus found his voice. 'Excuse me for not coming from a sink estate and being the product of a lesbian mother and an alcoholic father,' he said. 'I suppose you'd prefer that.'

'It'd make more bloody sense.'

Rufus raised his eyebrows with some effort. 'Well, well, who'd have thought it. Nutters can be bigots too.'

'I'm no chuffing bigot!'

'No? Is that why you've condemned me without knowing anything about me? My voice offends you, my money offends you, and that's it, is it? All bets are off. I'm a rich fucker who has no business being ill. Congratulations, Miss West Yorkshire, you've succeeded where many have failed in here. You've actually managed to surprise me. I thought, and this must prove how mad I am, that a person who knew what it was like to be a nutter from personal experience might just possibly have the teeniest bit of insight into what it was like for someone else. And that same person might be different from all the ignorant bastards who've been telling me to pull myself together and admit how blessed I am all these fucking years. But no, how wrong I was. Everywhere I go it's the same. Privileged plus posh, plus depressed, equals whingeing failure. Dragged up in a high rise by parents with a combined IQ of room temperature, plus packs of feral children to play with, plus any fucking psychosis you like, equals poor unfortunate deserving of our sympathy. Now I know what they mean by the NHS being a postcode lottery.'

Kate had found herself uncharacteristically lost for words. She had settled for a sneer and tightly folded arms. It had been days before she had spoken to him again, but he had touched a nerve. She had been forced to admit to herself, even in the treacly darkness of her own depression, that he had a point. She had her own prejudices. Her own unjust assumptions. Rufus had shown her that.

'Fruit Juice and Dairy Products,' a voice broke into Kate's thoughts.

She turned to find Lindy, Quickshopper's youngest and smiliest employee beaming at her.

'You what?'

'Mr Morgan asked me to tell you. You're needed in...'

'...Fruit Juice and Dairy Products. OK. I got it.' Kate slid the last box of Smooth 'n' Silky into place and headed off for aisle seven with a heartfelt sigh.

CHAPTER FOUR

The waiting room at Dr Spinks's surgery was, like the man himself, refined, elegant, and quietly fabulous. Rufus sat on one of the modish but comfortable chairs and tired hard to resist the seductive charm of the place. The walls were painted a soothing shade of marine blue, pale enough to be light reflecting, bold enough to evoke a calm Pacific. On these walls hung tasteful paintings, all originals, far too modern and cutting-edge to be of anything recognisable, and yet they were undeniably clever and appealing. A hard act to pull off, Rufus knew. He had sometimes managed to come across as clever but this had, apparently, always rendered him unappealing. Did one have to be stupid to be loved? Was that it? No, that wouldn't work with his mother, he reminded himself. The oceanic theme, more symbolic than seafaring, continued with artfully placed pieces of bleached driftwood and black and white photographs of windblown sand dunes. The furnishings were either turquoise or white, and the Axminster a deep ultramarine with tiny cerulean shells dotted at considered random. The main focus of the room was a tropical aquarium of impressive proportions. No broken bridges or plastic shipwrecks littered the bottom of this little glimpse of underwater paradise. Instead exquisite corals and sea plants glowed and waved gently in the artificial current while all manner of exotic fish darted among the fronds. Although clearly designed to attract attention, Rufus found the piece somehow too lovely, too beautiful, too darn perfect for people with troubled and considerably less-than-perfect minds to have to cope with. The room was finished off with an abundance of wispy ferns and exotic blooms of great beauty and no doubt greater expense. Not a drooping spider-plant in sight. Behind the reception desk (of palest scrubbed oak) sat Marion, as unfathomably gorgeous as any mermaid. Through hidden speakers came muted sounds of softly breaking waves and rustling palm leaves. Rufus wondered if the day would soon arrive when girls in grass skirts would be employed to serve coconut milk.

He picked up a glossy magazine and flicked blindly through it. The room had been designed to calm and reassure, but it could do nothing to dispel the effects the patients within in it had upon one another. A young woman sat clutching a box of tissues and weeping silently. An elderly man with an impressive beard stood at the window, muttering ceaselessly to himself. A middle-aged couple sat beside each other without touching, the tension between them forming an almost tangible barrier. Not for the first time, Rufus wondered how any supposedly sane person could choose to spend his working life facing one desperate client after another, day in day out. The money must have helped. And the power, perhaps. After all, to these people Dr Spinks was God, Daddy, Knight In Shining Armour, and Obernfüuhrer of the Thought Police all rolled into one personable, attractive package. You wouldn't get the same mixture of respect and terror working in advertising. Or the City. Or anywhere Rufus could imagine.

The longer he was forced to sit and wait, the less able he was to contain his mounting agitation. He knew he had been lucky to obtain a precious Saturday afternoon appointment at such short notice. He also knew he would be charged handsomely for it. If he'd wanted to spend hours in waiting rooms he would not have engaged a private psychiatrist. His left knee began to jig up and down. He dropped the magazine back on the table and closed his eyes. He remembered his very first therapy session. He remembered it even more clearly than his very first sexual experience, in fact, which was worrying in itself. He had been only fifteen, and his leg had twitched in a similar way on both occasions. His first therapist was a stout woman with a bubble perm and outsized earrings. She wore no make up, save for a slick of poorly applied crimson lipstick which served to emphasise her thin perma-smile. Both she and Rufus sat on corduroy-covered beanbags. He remembered the long silences, broken only by the irritating rustling of the polystyrene beads as he attempted to find a comfortable yet dignified position. At last he could stand it no longer.

'Aren't you supposed to ask me something?' he wanted to know.

'What questions would you like me to ask, Rufus?' the counsellor spoke softly.

'Well, not that one for a start.'

There was another interminable pause.

'I don't know what you want me to say,' Rufus tried again.

'This is your time, Rufus. You tell me whatever it is that you want to tell me.'

Another chasm of silence opened up in the middle of the room.

Rufus shook his head, 'Fuck knows why this is called psychodynamic counselling. Can't see anything sodding dynamic about it. Nothing happens!'

'I'm sensing anger, Rufus.'

'Thank fuck for that. I was beginning to think you were a hologram.'

'Do holograms worry you, Rufus?'

'No, of course they bloody don't. You finally come up with a question and it's something totally ludicrous.'

The counsellor wrote in the notepad on her lap. 'And how does that make you feel?' she asked gently.

'Like this is the complete waste of time I knew it would be.'

She nodded and scribbled some more, then returned to watching Rufus, the thin smile never wavering.

'I'm not mad, you know,' Rufus said. 'I only agreed to see you because my mother made me. I'm no nutter.'

'Is that how you think people see you, Rufus? As a nutter?'

'No.'

'Is that why you ran away from school, Rufus?'

'No!'

'Is that why you tried to hurt yourself?'

'No!!'

Rufus opened his eyes and shook away the memory. He was alarmed to find Marion standing in front of him. Someone so distractingly beautiful should be more careful about sneaking up on people, he felt. He pressed his palm firmly down on his jiggling knee to steady it.

'Mr Waters?' her smile revealed impossibly perfect teeth. 'Dr Spinks will see you now.'

Dr Spinks's room was another triumph of stylish modern décor. It was large and comfortable, with a sofa, but nothing that could accurately be called a couch. There were several designer leather chairs, a well-stocked bookshelf, a large window, and an imposingly broad desk sporting a writing pad, a family photo, and a lump of green glass that could have been a paperweight, had there been any paper so recklessly free as to require pinning down.

Dr Graham Ellory Spinks had about him a charm so faultless, so seemingly natural and sincere, it was dangerous. He must have been in his late fifties, but he was a fine example of what healthy living and good grooming could do for a man. He wore his abundant salt and pepper hair long enough to be romantic and daring, his neatly trimmed beard softening the look. His china blue eyes found their target and locked on like Exocet missiles, allowing no escape from his charm offensive. As he stood up and extended a hand towards Rufus his Armani suit adjusted itself perfectly to reveal discreet but dazzling amber links on starched, chalk-white cuffs. When he spoke his slow Toronto drawl flavoured every word with a casual friendliness.

'Hey, Rufus! Good to see you.' He pumped Rufus's clammy hand. 'Sit down, sit down. You want coffee? I'll get Marion to bring some in.' He pressed the switch on the intercom. 'Could you fix us some of your very best coffee, please, Marion? Wonderful.' He let go of the switch and smiled warmly before sitting down behind his desk. He leaned back in his chair, his head slightly on one side, his eyes never for one second releasing Rufus from their hypnotic hold. 'So,' he gestured at his face, 'you've taken up boxing?'

Rufus perched on the edge of his chair. 'Look, I won't mess about,' he said, 'I've come here to tell you that I won't be coming. Any more. Here. To see you.' He paused, expecting a strong reaction to this news. Dr Spinks merely raised his eyebrows, put his fingertips together, and nodded. Rufus marvelled at the gesture. Did they teach them to do that at Shrink School? Was there a little repertoire of infuriating and patronising responses they had to perfect before they got licensed to shrink? And were they all trained not to react in any way to any news however big, however important? For God's sake, *he* was the one who was supposed to be abnormal. How was this a normal response? Rufus pressed on. 'The thing is, I've had enough of all this. The whole mental health thing. So, I've decided. Enough is enough. No more drugs. No more therapy. No more you.'

'That's very interesting, Rufus. Don't worry, I won't take it personally.'

'Oh? Perhaps you should.'

'You think so?'

'Why not?'

'OK, so it's personal. You don't want to talk to me any more. Would you like to talk to someone else, maybe?'

'No thank you. I don't want to talk to anyone. I'm done with talking.'

Marion arrived with the coffee. She set the tray down on the desk, exchanging glamorous smiles with Dr Spinks.

'Here we are,' he said. 'Thank you so much, Marion. That smells terrific.' He watched her leave, making Rufus feel for a moment that he had forgotten he was in the room. 'I'd be lost without her, you know,' he said at last. 'Great girl. Now, where were we? No more me, and no more drugs you say?'

'That's right.'

'Cream in your coffee? Sugar?'

Rufus nodded.

Dr Spinks dropped two lumps into the fine white cup. 'Glad to see you're not giving up all drugs,' he said with a tiny laugh.

Rufus resisted the urge to sneer. 'Who knows,' he said, 'I may take up some new ones. Cocaine, perhaps. Or heroin. But no more of your prescribed rubbish. You hear?'

'Oh I hear you, Rufus. I hear you.'

They drank their coffee in silence for a moment until Rufus said, 'And I plan to get a job.'

'Is that so? Good for you!'

'Yes, so, there it is.'

'There it is,' Dr Spinks agreed.

Rufus finished his coffee, set down his cup and saucer and stood up. 'So, goodbye then,' he said, turning to leave.

'Oh Rufus,' Dr Spinks called after him, 'I'm curious.'

'Yes?'

'Do you want to be well so you can get a job, or do you want a job so you can be well? Which is it, d'you think? Only, it's never bothered you before, not working. Strikes me you've always been quite happy living off your inheritance up till now. What changed, I wonder? Does it have anything to do with that truly magnificent black eye you have there? Or is it for your father, Rufus? Do you think this is what he would have wanted? Is that why you feel you have to do all this on your own, without any help? To prove yourself to him, maybe?'

Rufus opened his mouth to speak. He wanted to say that his father, had he lived, would probably have just taken him fly-fishing every Sunday and left it at that. He wanted to say that this wasn't about anyone else, it was about him, about his life, about how it felt for him to be laughed at and marginalized and pitied. He wanted to explain that he wanted people to stop looking at him with exactly the expression with which Dr Spinks was regarding him now, but what was the point? If Rufus hadn't been a nutter Dr Spinks would not have been looking at him at all. Perhaps he wasn't truly keen on Rufus becoming sane, because if he did he would be of no interest to him any more.

'Goodbye, Dr Spinks,' he said, and made his escape.

'My door is always open to you, Rufus,' Dr Spinks called as he went. 'Always open!'

By the time Rufus arrived at his brother's house that evening he was beginning to feel more than a little weary. The combination of not enough sleep and nothing at all in the way of his usual medication was starting to show. It was with some relief that he reached the reassuringly scruffy front door of the large, shabby, red brick vicarage, most of which was almost entirely obscured by climbing plants. He ignored the bell that had never, to his knowledge, actually worked, and knocked firmly.

Matthew appeared, grubby glasses half way down his nose, his thinning hair as always giving the impression he had just encountered freak weather of some sort, his favourite green cardigan sporting yet another hole, and his slippers showing evidence of further episodes of distressing by Labrador teeth. Indeed, the only thing about his brother that was in any way kempt and smart-looking was his dog collar. Rufus liked the way Matthew's appearance seemed to so accurately reflect his brother's view of the importance of things, and the order of things, and the way life should be lived. He knew that, unlike his brother, he himself could only dream of such a stable and comforting shape to his own existence.

Matthew beamed over his specs, 'Hello there, baby brother. You're nice and early. Gracious, whatever has happened to you?'

'Don't ask.'

'Fair enough. Come along then, in you come. Helen's in the kitchen working her magic.'

They picked their way through the chaos of a hallway which could have been wide and spacious had it not been home to scores of pairs of boots, pegs groaning under the weight of a dozen coats, each more moth-eaten than the last, numerous walking sticks and umbrellas, and endless fishing paraphernalia. The kitchen was almost as cluttered, but its size at least allowed room for movement. Helen stood at the Aga, leaning forwards so as not to disturb the sleeping dog at her feet. She was a woman for whom the word 'homely' might have been invented. Her plumpness gave away her fondness for food, her clothes spoke of comfort with whispers of jollity, her rosy skin was untroubled by make-up, and her mousy hair frizzed unchecked.

'Hello,' she called through the steam, then, glancing up at Rufus, 'Hell's teeth! What happened to you?'

'He doesn't want to talk about it,' Matthew told her.

'Right you are. Where's my kiss, then?' Spoon in hand she proffered a dimpled cheek. Rufus kissed her, but not without stepping on the slumbering Labrador. 'Oops!' Helen laughed. 'Mind poor old Henry. Silly creature will insist on sitting there. My goodness, Rufus, you get thinner every time I see you.'

'Always hungry for one of your meals, Helen.'

Matthew pressed a bundle of cutlery into his hands. 'Have to work for your supper around here, you know,' he said. 'Remember where the dining room is, do you?'

Rufus heard the front door open and shut. He raised his brows.

'Ahh,' Matthew shuffled away, not meeting his brother's eye. 'That'll be Mummy.'

'You never told me she was coming.'

'Didn't I mention it?'

Rufus caught the scent of warm mint and salty butter as Helen squeezed by with a large bowl of potatoes.

'Cheer up, sweet thing. I've got a couple of bottles of her favourite standing by to put her in a sunny mood,' she told him.

'Good luck with that,' he said. 'Last time I saw her in a sunny mood was when she thought they might bring back capital punishment.'

Matthew pushed him towards the far door. 'Go and lay the table and leave her to me.'

In keeping with the rest of the house the dining room was filled to overflowing. A table that might once have had pretensions to grandeur now struggled beneath stacks of the Church Times, Herefordshire Living, and coffee-stained copies of the Parish Magazine. The mirror above the fireplace reflected the backs of a score of aged postcards from holidays of several seasons ago, and invitations to functions long forgotten. Rufus cleared half the table and set out the knives and forks. He unearthed some place mats depicting the Cathedrals of England, and positioned two lightly tarnished candlesticks centre stage. He was doing his best not to let his shoulders slump. The idea of a quiet and delicious supper with Matthew and Helen had seemed manageable. The prospect of an evening with his mother was another thing altogether. He resolved to be cheerful and upbeat. He refused to let her browbeat him. Not this time. Not now, when he was so focused, so determined, so fixed on his plan.

As the family took their seats at the table Helen slipped a CD into the machine. Frank Sinatra sang of ants, effortlessly making them rhyme with rubber plants.

'You don't mind if Frank joins us, do you? I do so love his voice.' Helen sat next to Rufus. 'Come along, come along. If you don't eat every last scrap I shall take offence and never set foot in the kitchen again.'

Rufus helped himself to slices of home-baked ham. 'It all looks splendid, as always, Helen,' he told her.

Lydia waved away the potatoes. 'And so much of it,' she said. Matthew went to fill her wine glass but she shook her head. 'Not for me, thank you.'

'No?'

'It's a Chilean Voignier,' Helen pointed out. 'The one you like.'

'I'm driving.'

Matthew kept the bottle poised. 'One little glass perhaps?'

'I think not. I realise self-control is out of vogue these days, but I must do as my conscience dictates.' She shot Rufus a glance. 'How is your face now?'

'Much better, thank you. Pass the piccalilli, would you? Nobody makes it quite like Helen.'

Matthew put down the bottle and leaned close to his mother. 'I think he'd rather not talk about it,' he said.

'Hardly surprising,' said Lydia. 'Brawling in a sleazy public house is not something one would want to brag about.'

Rufus tried to keep his voice light. 'I did not "brawl".'

Helen looked shocked. 'Gracious. Were you attacked?'

Lydia was quick to explain, 'Some oaf called him nasty

52

names, so Rufus thumped him. Really. The behaviour of the school ground.'

'Please, Mummy, let's just drop it, shall we? It really is nothing to do with you.'

'Oh? Is that why I found myself at the police station in the small hours on your behalf?'

Matthew inhaled his wine. 'Police station?'

Lydia went on, 'Not content with embarrassing himself in front of a roomful of strangers, your brother succeeded in getting himself arrested. Still, I was only glad I could help, of course. One likes to be useful.'

Rufus heard a faint twanging sound as his nerves began to fray. 'If I'd known another solicitor I would have called them, believe me,' he said.

'Are they going to press charges?' Matthew wanted to know.

Rufus shook his head.

Helen did her best to lighten the tone, 'Well, that's that then. No real damage done. More Greek beans, anyone?'

'Thank you, Helen.' Rufus took the bowl from her. 'And I'll have another drop of that rather nice wine, seeing as it's going begging.'

Lydia narrowed her eyes. 'Perhaps you should try a little abstinence yourself, Rufus.'

'I wasn't drunk when I hit that lout.'

'No? What was your excuse, then?'

'I told you, I am not taking any more rubbish from anyone about being a sodding nutter. OK? In fact, I went to see Dr Spinks today. Told him I won't be requiring his services any longer.'

Matthew and Helen paused in their eating, forks suspended.

'Oh?' Matthew waited.

'Nor will I be taking any more of his silly little pills,' Rufus added.

His brother and sister-in-law exchanged worried looks. Matthew put down his fork and picked up his wineglass. 'You're going to stop your medication? Just like that?'

'Dear Heart, do you think that's wise?' Helen asked.

'I think it's the sanest thing I've done in years. There's no need to look at me as if I've got my head on back to front. I know what I'm doing.'

Matthew gulped Voignier. Helen toyed with her potatoes.

Lydia gave Rufus a fierce frown. 'For Heaven's sake, Rufus, what is the matter with you? It's just one irresponsible act after another. You can't possibly believe you know better that your extremely well-qualified, and I might add extremely expensive, psychiatrist. Why must you persist in this sort of self-destructive behaviour? Will you stop at nothing to gain attention?'

'Mummy,' Matthew put in, 'I think you're being a bit harsh.'

'Oh, really, Matthew. You are much too soft on your brother. You always have been. It just encourages him to be... There is such a thing as being too sympathetic, you know.'

Rufus gave a bark of a laugh. 'We wouldn't want anything like *sympathy* going on, now, would we? Heaven forfend. Poor old Dad never saw any of it when he was ill. Our wretched step-father didn't know how lucky he was, dropping dead on the treadmill. And as for me and Matthew when we were kids, forget it. Would it have killed you to show us you cared how we were feeling?'

'I did the best I could. It wasn't easy for me either.'

'You don't say.'

'Sometimes I think you actually blame me for your condition.'

'My condition? Let's call a spade an excavating implement, shall we? I am a depressive. And you can't handle the fact. I've been an embarrassment to you all my adult life. Well, worry no more, Mother. I've decided you were right all along. All I need to do is pull myself together. Get a grip and get on with it. Show some backbone. Peace of piss! Can't think why I haven't tried it before.'

There was a painful silence, broken only by the sound of Rufus's fork on his plate as he continued to eat, and Frank singing on undaunted in the background. Rufus chomped on with renewed determination. 'This really is excellent ham, Helen. Excellent.'

Matthew gave up all pretence at eating and drained his glass. Even Helen's appetite seemed to have dimmed. Lydia pushed her plate away.

Frank's words filled the room.

'*He's got high hopes! High hopes! High in the pie in the sky hopes!*'

Later, Rufus walked home along the darkened riverbank feeling strangely pleased with himself. Standing up to his mother was something of a new experience for him. Having done so gave him hope. After all, if he could convince her that the New Improved Rufus Waters was in town, how hard could anything else be?

The clouds of earlier in the evening had drifted away to reveal a clear night sky spangled with optimistic stars. The river flowed gently on. Amid the grasses at the water's edge, a bank vole foraged for food, whiskers twitching. Rufus smiled at it. Small but indomitable. Vulnerable but fearless. He applauded its spirit. As he looked on, the little animal froze mid step, as if sensing danger. A movement above caused Rufus to start. In a heartbeat a barn owl had descended, talons outstretched, snatched up the vole, and borne it away into the darkness. A chill travelled down Rufus's spine. He turned up the collar of his jacket and hurried on.

That night he slept badly. The hours stretched before him. His bed became a thing of stones. By the small hours his bedclothes were drenched in sweat. When at last the alarm clock sounded to warn him of the awakening day Rufus was in no mood for it. He threw the offending device across the room, pulled a pillow over his head, and continued his quest for sleep.

CHAPTER FIVE

Kate sat on the park bench lobbing stale bread to the eager ducks and pigeons at her feet. The morning was dry and warm, but the brightness had gone out of the sunshine a little; the blue of the sky faded. Teach stood at a nearby bin, peering inside, absent-mindedly chewing on a crust of wholemeal that had been intended for the birds. Kate frowned and threw a piece of hardened cake in his direction. It hit him smartly on his bony brow.

'My word!' he clutched his head dramatically. 'That's a powerful overarm you have there, Kate. Have you ever considered taking up cricket?'

'Stop rummaging and come and talk to me.'

Teach did as she asked, arranging himself uncomfortably on the bench beside her, his collecting bags at his feet. 'Could have been an interesting demise – felled by a scone. Aeschylus was killed by a tortoise striking him on the noggin. Did you know that?'

'Can't say as I did.'

'The story goes that an eagle had caught the hapless tortoise and was flying home with it.'

'Like a Greek takeaway?'

'Precisely so. Anyhow, said eagle had a system for opening the aforementioned reptile which involved dropping it on a large stone. Spotting old Aeschylus's bald pate he let go, and the thing plummeted to earth, bouncing off the scribe's bonce on the way down. Seriously unlucky. For him and the tortoise.'

'Well I feel sorry for the eagle. Imagine the grief he must have got arriving home with nothing for tea.'

'You know, I don't think I ever stopped to consider the ramifications for the bird.'

The two sat for a moment as the squabbling fowl pecked at crumbs at their feet. Kate fidgeted.

'Rufus missed choir practice yesterday,' she said.

'Really? Not like our Ruf, is it?'

Kate paused, searching for the words. She wanted to talk about what Rufus was doing. Needed to. And, after all, Teach was probably the best, chuff it, the only person she could safely share her thoughts with. It wasn't just about Rufus. She knew it, and Teach would understand that too. It was about all of them.

'D'you think he can do it?' she asked at last.

'Sorry?'

'Rufus. This whole think-yourself-sane business. Has he got a snowball's chance?'

Teach shrugged slowly, the sharp bones of his shoulders raising his worn jacket into points. '*Audaces fortuna iuvat,*' he assured her.

'You what?'

'Fortune favours the brave.'

'Oh aye? And how does Fortune feel about the plain chuffing stupid?'

'It's good that he's prepared to give it a go.'

'You think?'

'Don't you?'

'I don't know.' She dug at a piece of shrivelled gum with the toe of her Dr Martin boot. It stuck stubbornly to the tarmac path. She stared at it while she spoke. 'I do know he's not as strong as he makes out. It could go badly wrong, couldn't it?'

Teach reached over and put a weightless hand on her sleeve. 'Let's give him a chance,' he said. 'He knows where we are if he needs us.'

A thoughtful silence was interrupted by the sound of the city clock striking eleven. Teach hurried to his feet.

'Good Lord, is that the time? I must away,' he said.

'What's the rush?'

'I'm seeing the quack at a quarter past.'

'Oh?'

Teach patted his chest. 'He wants to give the old pump the once over.'

'Again?'

'Seems he thinks I should be long dead, judging by the sorry state of my innards.' Teach picked up his bags and backed away, rustling, as he spoke. 'You see before you a walking miracle. A wonder of modern medicine!' He gave an expressive wave with his left arm while continuing backwards, completely failing to see a poorly parked wheelie bag belonging to an elderly lady on the next bench. Teach tripped, teetered, arms flailing, then fell in an undignified heap, apologizing all the while to both the bag and its owner.

Kate half rose, concerned that such brittle bones would surely snap at the slightest provocation, but Teach was scrambling to his feet. He waved back to Kate.

'I'm OK. No harm done. *Mea culpa*. Pride before a fall, and all that.'

She watched him go, the smile of farewell fading on her face. Teach looked so fragile, but, she wondered, which one of them was really most at risk? It was just not like Rufus to miss choir practice. He might be a useless beggar at most things, but he loved his music, and he had a passable voice. He must be unwell. She stood up, suddenly concerned, and strode towards the footbridge.

Ten minutes later she was ringing Rufus's doorbell. After pressing it for the third time she pushed open the letterbox and squinted through. What she could see of the flat looked to be in its usual state of casual neglect.

'Rufus?' she called through the narrow slit. 'Get your lazy arse out of bed. The day's half done. What are you doing in there? Rufus!'

She let the flap fall and put her ear to the door. At last she began to make out muffled noises. The door opened. Rufus stood in tee-shirt and boxers, looking pasty.

'Where the bloody hell were you?' Kate demanded. 'You've missed choir practice completely this time, you useless article.'

'Good morning to you, too, Kate,' said Rufus, retreating towards the kitchen.

Kate followed him. 'It won't do, you know. Your absence was noticed. We've a chuffing concert only a few weeks away. You'll get chucked out if you don't watch it.'

'You're mistaking me for someone who cares.' Rufus filled the kettle and lit the gas ring beneath it, before leaning against the sink and running his hands through his chaotic hair.

'You do care,' Kate said. 'You know you do. Singing is about the only thing you can be bothered with, as far as I know. Or have you taken up a new hobby to go with your lovely new sane life? Sumo wrestling, perhaps?'

'If you must know, I'm thinking about giving it up. I don't know if the choir is the right thing for me to be doing at the moment.' He busied himself taking mugs from the draining board.

Kate pulled at his arm, making him face her. 'Any choir? Or *this* choir in particular?'

'What?'

'Maybe Rufus The Normal doesn't want to be part of a choir made up mostly of loonies.'

'That has nothing to do with it. I've just got a lot of other things to think about at the moment. That's all.'

Kate opened her mouth to reply but thought better of it. Into the silence came the sound of the whistling kettle. For a moment neither of them moved. Rufus held her gaze, but Kate could not read his expression. She let go his arm. He turned, relieved, it seemed, that she was prepared to let the subject drop.

'Tea or coffee?' he asked.

Kate shook her head and began walking towards the door. 'No, ta,' she said. 'I'll be late for work.' On her way out she paused. 'I just came to check,' she said. 'Just to make sure you're, you know, OK.'

Rufus nodded. 'I am,' he said. 'I am OK.'

'You look like shite,' she told him.

He laughed a little, the tension broken. 'No change there then,' he said, then added, 'I'll see you at The Grapes tonight, yeah?'

Kate looked at him standing half dressed, steam from the kettle still billowing about him. For such a tall man he looked strangely insubstantial. As if he could be whipped up in the cloud of water vapour and disappear with it through the air vent in the wall in an instant. She felt a sudden sadness grip her, though she did not understand why.

'Yeah,' she said, trying a smile but not putting much heart into it. 'See you at The Grapes, then.'

It had been Rufus who had introduced Kate to the delights of the pub they now called their local. Being in the city centre it was often filled with transient tourists or shoppers pausing for refreshment, but there was still a hard core of regulars. Kate, Rufus and Teach were among the most loyal. The interior had successfully resisted all attempts at modernisation and remained happily traditional, from its dark brown beams and woodwork, to its swirly red and green carpet and brass fixtures and fittings. The bar bristled with taps offering an impressive selection of real ales. By the time Kate arrived that evening, Teach and Rufus were on the point of putting their first pints to their lips. She perched on a stool, for once able to see eye to eye with the men. Rufus bought her a pint of Theakston's Peculiar and the three supped quietly for a moment or two, savouring that first sip of the evening.

Kate wiped foam from her mouth with the back of her hand. 'So, Teach, what did the doctor say?'

'Oh, he did some tests. Said I'll have to wait a bit for the results. He was extremely thorough, I must say.'

'Got your money's worth then?'

'Absolutely. Mmm, this is an exceptionally good pint, Ruf.'

'Always tastes better when somebody else has paid for it,' Rufus said.

'You should know,' said Kate. 'You still look shite, by the way.'

'I didn't sleep well.'

'Aah,' Teach shook his head earnestly. 'It begins.'

'What begins?' Rufus took another swig of his rapidly disappearing beer.

'The process of weaning yourself from your chemical dependency, my friend.'

'You make me sound like a drug addict.'

'Aren't you?' Kate asked. 'Aren't we all?'

'Do you have to work at being provoking?' Rufus wanted to know. 'Or does it come naturally?'

Teach let out an appreciative belch. 'She has got a point there, Ruf,' he said. 'Your medication of choice may be of the legal and prescribed variety, but there are similarities to those substances of a more illicit ilk.'

'You'd know about that, Teach,' Rufus conceded.

'Indeed, I did not reach my current state of enlightenment, and, I'll admit, degeneration, without indulging in the recreational use of a smorgasbord of illegal substances over a considerable number of years.'

Kate signalled to the barmaid for a packet of Ready Salted. 'You must have gone cold turkey a few times yourself,' she said to Teach.

'I am no stranger to that frigid bird. And yes, it can be done. Of course the amount of suffering is directly proportionate to the potency of the substance from which one is endeavouring to escape. *Ipso facto*, the higher the trip, the lower the dip.' He poured a little more Dr Butterworth down his throat before continuing. 'Cocaine can be a viciously possessive mistress. Heroin, goes without saying, very unpleasant coming off that one. Though of course,' he pulled a packet of tobacco from his pocket and began to roll a cigarette as he spoke, 'it has now been proven that nicotine is the most addictive substance of all. Unless you count sugar. Personally I don't. Though you may want to, if you're giving up everything else. A craving for all things sweet is a common side effect of coming off mind altering medication.'

'Go on, Teach,' Kate popped open the packet and began to munch crisps, 'tell him what he's letting himself in for.'

'Ooh, let me see. To begin with, there's your Prozac – queen of the selective serotonin re-uptake inhibitors. She won't give you up without headaches, cold sweats, dry mouth... a little nausea, maybe. Plus the obvious psychological freefall as one's serotonin levels revert to their more natural erratic state. What else were you partaking of, Ruf? The occasional diazepam, no doubt? A necessary evil. Takes those sharp edges off a jagged world. Brace yourself for panic as everything is revealed to you in relentlessly crisp focus once again. Sleeping tablets? Thought so. Prepare for endless day, my friend. Amazing how completely one's body loses the ability to get to sleep on its own after only a short time of being chemically nudged into the arms of Morphy Richards.' Teach underlined his words of doom with another loud burp.

Rufus refused to be unnerved.

'Thank you so much for the information, Teach. All very fascinating, I'm sure. Now shut up and cough up. It's your round.'

'Not giving up alcohol then?' asked Kate.

'I plan to enjoy my new lifestyle. At least now I shall be able to have more than two pints without passing out. Come on, Teach, invest your disability allowance wisely.'

'Absolutely,' Teach fumbled in the lining of his jacket pocket. 'Same again, everyone? Must say, Ruf, might pay you to lie low for a week or two. Give the old process a chance to do its thing.'

'Can't be done, I'm afraid. I haven't the time. Things to do. People to see.'

Kate pulled a face. 'What things? What people?'

'If you must know, I've got an interview for a job. Tomorrow, in fact.'

'A job! You!' she laughed. 'Using which of your many and wonderful skills, exactly?'

'I'm not going to tell you any more about it until I've got the job. So sneer all you like.'

Teach was impressed. 'Brave stuff, Ruf. Here's good luck to you. Cheers!'

He raised his glass and bashed it against Rufus's freshly filled pint mug. Kate frowned, finding herself more than a little reluctant to join in the toast.

CHAPTER SIX

Later, as Teach had predicted, sleep eluded Rufus. He lay in bed listening to the rain splashing off the windows and thought nervously about what was to come. The odd headache and fuzziness of thought he could manage. Panic attacks were ghastly, but he had techniques for dealing with them and hopefully they would soon pass, once he got into his stride and got the hang of the whole sane-and-normal business. It was insomnia that truly frightened him. He knew only too well where it could lead. Was there any way of avoiding it, he wondered? Of somehow tricking his body and his psyche, so that they failed to notice what was going on? Distraction, that was the key. Perhaps he should go away for a week or two. A change of environment might be just the thing. But no, he had his interview, and, all things going to plan, a job. A series of snatched day trips, then. Outings. He could go with someone who might actually enjoy such things and know where to go. Helen sprang to mind. She had to be a member of National Heritage Gardens, or some such. Or he could take one of those coach trips that were always being advertised on posters around town. To the seaside, maybe. He shuddered as he was assailed by a sudden and vivid flashback to the last time he had stood on the beach. Only the year or so before. How could he have forgotten, even for a moment? Teach and Kate had been there too, but the three of them had, by unspoken agreement, never mentioned or alluded to the hateful experience since. Not once.

He remembered now that the whole ridiculous occasion had been the idea of some deluded member of staff at the Belmont. Beware do-gooders. They not only pave the road to hell with their good intentions, they drag you along it with them. It had been hot that August, and everyone had been complaining about the lack of air conditioning on the wards, and the limited time they were allowed to spend in the gardens. The corridors reeked of sweat even more than usual, and tempers, ordinarily frayed to fringes at best, were at snapping point. So, Well Meaning Nurse had talked to the Man In Charge, and after a couple of days of to-ing and fro-ing, a trip had been organised. A day out at the seaside. Weston-super-Mare. Rufus had been pleased. With most of the perspiring inmates (at least, those of a reasonably steady nature) away, he would have room to breathe. And as the place would be short staffed, no-one would notice if he took a good book, his iPod, and a bottle of mineral water, and settled himself in a shady spot beneath the copper beech for the day. He had felt quite chipper about the whole thing. His own date for leaving was, he believed, only a matter of a week or so away. This would help the time pass and give him a short period of respite from the whirling madness that was customary on the ward. However, it was not to be. His weekly meeting with Dr Meadows had not gone well, and there was a very real possibility that he would be kept in for another month at least. How could they do that to a person? Dangle freedom in front of them and then snatch it away at the last second? Had they no idea what havoc that played with an already fragile mind? Kate had found him sulking near the water cooler.

'Now then, Our Rufus, you planning to try and drown yourself in that, or what?' she asked.

'The thought had crossed my mind.'

'Chuffing selfish, as usual. What about our drinking facilities? Why should every beggar else be inconvenienced? Go and contaminate the fish-pond with your gloomy carcass.'

'I just might. I saw Meadows this morning. Says he's not happy I'm stable enough yet. They're not going to let me go home for another month. At least.'

'I heard.' She helped herself to a cup of water, giving the dispenser a good slap when it began to splutter. 'So,' she talked through her plastic cup as she sipped, ' you coming on the Belmont Beach Bonanza then?'

'You're going?' Rufus was incredulous.

'Bloody right I am. Pass up a chance to score serious Brownie points like that? You'd have to be mad.'

'You think he'll look favourably on our cases if we go? Show willing, join in, that sort of thing?' Now he was interested.

'Why else d'you think he agreed to it? Perfect way to spot the wobblers. And to see who's ready to be released back into the wild. If I were you, I'd be digging out my swimmies sharpish.'

And so it was that, on the only cloudy day there had been for weeks, a boisterous coach-load of inmates from the Belmont set off towards the sea. Rufus cringed as the first bout of enthusiastic singing began. He had chosen to sit near the front with Teach and Kate. Partly to distance himself from the jolly back-seaters, who had reverted from whatever mental age they might normally boast to a bunch of nine-year olds the minute they had stepped aboard. And partly to distract himself by watching the traffic on the motorway. He had never owned a car and rarely went out of Hereford. If he did, it was by train. He was, therefore, mesmerised by the swirling, whooshing, speeding vehicles. A crash of serious proportions seemed a foregone conclusion, and yet the coach driver merrily chewed gum and whistled, apparently at one with the Death Race his job entailed. Rufus thought the whole thing was utterly fascinating, rather like watching a building being demolished and wondering if you were standing too close. Or looking down from a tall building and contemplating what the descent might be like. Even so, he found himself wishing the driver would at least stop whistling, lest he choke on his gum. With all the juggernauts and Supercars that were trying to run them off the road, it was, he decided, taking multitasking to reckless levels. He shifted in his seat to glance behind him. There were around twenty merry day-trippers. A finer collection of neuroses and phobias it would be hard to find. One or two inmates sat alone, silent and white-knuckled. Another was already vomiting into a paper bag. A tall woman he didn't recognise was handing out barley sugars. The merriest among them were, unfortunately, intent on singing their way south. Even Mute Mavis, a long-term resident, was grinning and nodding her head. Their cheerleader was Belinda. Rufus had shared day room facilities with Belinda on several occasions. She was, like him, a depressive. A serial offender. Brought into the Belmont at irregular intervals to quell suicidal thoughts, readjust her serotonin levels, or just prevent her chiselling chunks out of herself. Again. To the uninformed she could easily pass herself off as a cheerful little housewife. She was in her fifties, short and stout. Her clothes, like her hair and her body, were shapeless, and yet there had clearly been thought and care put into her appearance. The dainty cubic zircona earrings. The pretty gold chain at her throat. The ill-advised pale blue eyeshadow. She had tried, at least. And, like many at a similar stage in what the medical profession liked to call 'recovery', she had perfected the art of pretending to be happy. Of course, it didn't fool the doctors, or the nurses, or the other inmates. But it would work on the public, when the time came she was permitted to move among them once more. This day out was the ideal opportunity for her to perform her pop-socks off. Good old Belinda. If luck was on her side, the cloud would thicken so that the long-sleeved blouse that so successfully covered the scars on her wrists would not draw puzzled looks on the beach.

Two of the nurses, one of them Well Meaning herself, who was to blame for the whole sorry event, the other a recent agency recruit, clapped along to the abysmal chorus of caterwauling. A burly male Jamaican nurse called Livingstone was deep in a copy of *The Mayor of Casterbridge*. A jittery young Polish member of the Home Treatment Team, who must have been in some way bullied or bribed to be there, fiddled with her mp3 player.

Rufus sighed and tried to get comfortable, tugging at the lever to his left. His seat flopped backwards so that he was reclining practically in Teach's lap. After muttered apologies he righted himself. He thought Teach was looking remarkably well. Well for him. Which meant skeletal, with a complexion the colour of putty, and hands trembling softly, causing the two, as yet empty, carrier bags he held to rustle like autumn leaves. At least his eyes had lost their popping-out appearance, his pupils relaxed to a near normal size, and his ceaseless sniffing, teeth sucking, and fidgeting had, for now, ceased. A fine example of the curative powers of the detox programme at the Belmont. Along with the anti-depressants and anti-psychotic medication that rattled inside him. Rufus found it hard to imagine Teach at the seaside. It would surely be too bright, too garish, too big, and loud, and real, and natural for his friend's frail body to withstand. Perhaps there would be a beach hut he could shelter in.

Across the aisle sat Kate, staring fixedly out of the window. For all her glibness and flippant comments, Rufus knew her to be struggling. He felt a surge of pity for her. He knew precisely where she was; at what point in her own lunatic cycle. It was the part where the two of them converged. Her darkness. Her low. The part of herself that was diametrically opposed to the flying, raving Kate who had been beaten down with a chemical cosh and tamed and calmed and brought to her psychological knees only a few months earlier. She looked exhausted. Worn out by the effort of clinging to the edge of that abyss. The doctors and therapists tested her, and checked her, and counselled her, and questioned her, and tweaked her medication this way and that. A smidge more lithium. A pinch more diazepam. Up the Prozac. Reduce the beta blockers. At least now she was out of reach of the nemesis of the unwillingly sectioned; Clopixel. Such a cruel drug. Effective, but at a price. Rufus had seen a man the size of an international prop forward come roaring onto the ward, flinging nurses, policemen and paramedics alike in all directions, as if they were made of balsa wood. He had watched as six, seven, then eight attendants had used all their weight and strength to pin him to the ground as he writhed, and bellowed, and thrashed, a water buffalo beset by crocodiles. Then the needle went in. The noise quietened. The energy that had entered the ward with the man evaporated, leaving nothing but the smell of fear and despair. A few hours later, with Clopixel working at its brutal best, that same man appeared, shuffling, dribbling, reduced to a heavy load of deadened humanity, inching his way up and down the corridors in a fruitless quest for God only knew what. Kate had endured just such an entrance to the Belmont. Again. Now, so many benumbed weeks later, the pharmaceutical veil had been lifted so that she might begin to live once more in the world, and to feel its pain. Like being born again, though not in some happy-clappy, evangelical way. Just raw and naked. No defences. No immunity. Poor Kate.

The journey turned out to be mercifully quick and uneventful, save for the fact that by the time they passed the sign welcoming them to Weston-super-Mare Rufus felt one more verse of *'Oh! Sir Jasper!'* would have had him begging for extreme tranquillisation himself. The small town was everything he expected it to be and less. The unattractive outskirts gave way to marginally more appealing suburbs, and then they were in the underwhelming town centre. All was as it should be. Ubiquitous chainstores. Shops with buckets and spades adorning their portals. Neapolitan flavoured houses. Bungalows with hydrangeas. The odd shivering palm. The coach swung into the car park and came to a hissing halt. The excited travellers, and Rufus, Kate, and Teach, were disgorged onto the tarmac.

Teach wriggled into his buff-coloured mac and stretched painfully, knees going off like rifle shots. 'Ahh, the

Englishness of it all,' he said. 'This was, for a short time, the home of the redoubtable Isambard Kingdom Brunel, did you know? The word "Weston" comes from the Anglo-Saxon for the west 'tun', or settlement,' he informed everyone. 'The descriptive addition to the name is, of course, medieval Latin. It translates literally as 'on sea'.

Kate snorted. 'It's not even chuffing *near* sea now. Look at it.'

They looked. She was right. This was, in fact, seaside for beginners, in as much as there was no sea. At least, none close enough to get wet in. The group stepped cautiously forward to the railings separating the vehicles from the beach itself. Ahead of them was a vast, open expanse of damp sand, relieved only by the subtle change in tone and colour where it turned into damp mud. Rufus thought he had never been anywhere that so aptly reflected his own inner emptiness. Behind him the agoraphobic began to whimper.

'Chuffing hell,' said Kate.

'Clearly no-one thought to check the tide times,' Rufus said, frowning pointedly at Well Meaning. 'Or the weather forecast,' he added, pulling his old leather jacket tighter around him against the chill wind that had begun to blow in off the Bristol Channel. The sun, it seemed, had also gone on a daytrip somewhere. A sock-grey sky hung heavily over the thin line of sock-grey sea on the horizon.

'Never mind!' Belinda would not be downhearted. Not if it killed her. Which well it might. 'I'm sure there's lots to do and see. And smell that wonderful, fresh sea air!' She spread her arms wide, puffed out her bulging bosom and inhaled half of Weston. Someone let it be known they needed the toilet. Several others thought this easily the best activity that might be on offer, and half the group trotted off in search of a public convenience. Well Meaning, with unconvincing help from Agency, marshalled the remaining huddle.

'Come on, everyone, let's get some sand between our toes. We can have a little walk and then some of our picnic. And there's the pier a bit further down. We could see what that has to offer.' She herded the more biddable patients towards the beach. Teach hung back. A keen south-westerly gust hit him hard and he looked as if he could be blown of his feet at any moment. His carrier bags filled with air like windsocks.

'I fancy there must surely be a tolerable hostelry close by in such a magnet for day-trippers as this. What say you, fellow travellers?'

Rufus and Kate did not need to be asked twice. The three slipped away, darted down a side street, and into the nearest pub they could find.

The Butcher's Arms was reassuringly similar in style, size, and indeed patrons, to The Bunch of Grapes. Rufus felt instantly at home. Which instantly made him feel homesick. He rebuked himself for the ridiculousness of this and allowed Teach to buy the first round.

'So much for bringing my bikini,' Kate said.

Rufus stared at her, her clothes magically falling off to reveal the body he had once known so well. He blinked away the unsettling vision. 'There's no way I am removing so much as a shoe out there,' he said. 'It's grim. Grimmer than grim, in fact. Grimmer, even, than the Belmont.'

Teach nodded. 'A suitably miserable greyness does seem to have descended,' he said, slurping his pint with relish.

Kate frowned at him. 'Hang about. Aren't you supposed to be on the wagon?'

'In point of fact,' he told her, 'I have indeed been aboard that conveyance of the sober and the clean. For some weeks. At the behest of the good Doctor Meadows and his team. Very pleasant fellow, can't fault him. Can't say I share his enthusiasm for abstinence though.' He belched loudly to underline his point. 'Naturally, I see the benefits of a brief period of abstaining from recreational drugs and alcohol.' He patted his chest and flexed his non-existent muscles. 'I stand before you evidence of the efficacy of that system. However, I am with Monsieur Descartes on this one.'

'How so?' asked Rufus.

'*Cogito ergo sum* – which loosely translates as "I drink, therefore I am".' He drained his pint mug and banged it on the table. 'Ready for the next?'

The trio spent an hour in the cosy seclusion of the public bar, embraced by the dim light of their surroundings and the comforting fuzziness of alcohol. Kate squinted through the window.

'It's brightening up out there. We'd best go and find the others. No point in going through all this just to get told off.'

Rufus knew she was right. He reluctantly wriggled back into his jacket. Teach got unsteadily to his feet.

'Just nipping into the Gents,' he told them.

After he had gone Kate scowled at Rufus.

'You shouldn't encourage him to drink.'

'What? Me? I don't see you swigging orange juice.'

'I'm not matching him pint for pint though, am I? He's out of practice. Needs to take it a bit slowly. Least until he gets his sea legs back.'

Rufus was about to point out that his recovery depended on him not drinking on a regular basis. A few pints now and again might be all right, but frequent bingeing was dangerous. But there was no point. They both knew Teach would go right back to living as he always had. And in a few months, or maybe a year, he'd hit bottom again, and another bit of him would wither, and he'd return to the Belmont and go through detox, and the whole process would start over.

After ten minutes Kate was getting seriously restless.

'Go and see what's happened to him.'

'Must I?'

'Well I can't, can I, you daft beggar?'

Rufus found the Gents empty. A high window banged in the breeze. He went back to Kate.

'He's legged it,' he told her.

'Chuffing great. Come on.'

'Come on where?'

'It's no good just standing there looking wet, we've got to find him before he gets himself into bother. Before they realise he's done a bunk.'

Rufus rolled his eyes and followed her out of the pub. Despite Kate's update on the weather there was still no discernible sun, and the wind continued to blow. Glum-looking holiday-makers milled about, but there was no sign of Teach.

'Where do we start?' Rufus wailed.

'Easy,' Kate strode off along a sloping side road, 'look for the cleanest streets.'

She had a point. Teach was not hard to track. A bin that had been sifted here. A carton-free stretch of pavement in front of a fried chicken takeaway there. The streets narrowed. Soon they were well off the main drag and edging towards a light industrial estate.

'There!' Kate shouted, pointing at the droopy figure exiting up an alleyway ahead. They hurried after him. They arrived at the entrance to the insalubrious pathway in time to see Teach, bulging bags at his feet, handing over a wad of money to a stringy youth in low-slung jeans.

'Teach!' Rufus called to him.

The youth grabbed the money and fled. Teach turned and acknowledged his friends with a cheerful wave.

'Good news!' he announced. 'I have acquired an interesting sample of local produce. When in Rome, cetera, cetera. Here, Ruf, fancy a little of this to lift your day?' he asked, proffering a small twist of paper containing a white powder of indeterminable provenance, and a palmful of pills.

Rufus shook his head. 'We should get back to the others. We'll be missed.'

'Absolutely. Grant me a moment to administer my *material medica*.' He fumbled with the wrap, pinching a generous couple of sniffs as if it were snuff. He put the remainder of the powder in his mac pocket and munched down three of the pills. 'Argh,' he grimaced, 'a little on the bitter side, but there we are. *De gustibus*... blah, blah, blah; no accounting for taste, and all that. Might be best washed down with another drop of Dr Butterworth?'

'No,' said Kate firmly, turning on her heel and leading them back to the seafront.

They found the others sitting on the beach only a few yards from the car park. The agoraphobic huddled in the centre of the group.

'There you are!' there was no missing the edge in Well Meaning's voice, but Rufus chose to ignore it.

Belinda stood up. 'Come along, come along,' she flapped

about thrusting tubs of this and that under their noses. 'Such lovely food. Don't be shy, now. Tuck in.'

Kate helped herself to a packet of crisps and sat a little way off from everyone else, facing out to sea. Teach took a chicken leg and settled on top of his bags, rabbiting on to himself incoherently as he nibbled. Rufus fought the urge to run back to the pub. He was very afraid people might start singing again. Mute Mavis was standing in the middle of one of the picnic rugs, swaying gently, gazing out at the distant water. Livingstone was chatting up the Polish girl, wooing her with mini pork pies. Brian from C ward had his cardigan over his head. Agency was dishing out tablets to the tall woman with the barley sugars. Rufus was on the point of inventing a plausible reason for heading off somewhere on his own, when he became aware that they were being watched. A nearby family was also eating an early lunch. Mummy doled out neat little sandwiches while the three small children busied themselves in the sand, and Daddy made minute adjustments to the windbreak. For a moment Rufus felt a strange solidarity with them. They were, after all, enduring a British holiday, on a British beach, in all-too-typically British weather, and making the best of it. Which is what his lot were trying to do. But then he noticed that Daddy was not, in fact, paying any attention to the flapping nylon he was supposed to be attending to. And Mummy was handing out food without seeing which sandy little hand took it. They were both watching the Belmont bunch. Not even discreetly. They were staring. Spectating, even. As if he and the others were some sort of bizarre seaside entertainment. The circus had come to town. Look at the loons! See the man who thinks he has two heads! Marvel at the woman who holds the record for the highest number of electric shock treatments! Gaze in wonder at the man who can only walk forwards in odd numbered paces! Shudder with horror at the lobotomy scars to your right, and the skin of the woman who scrubs herself with Brillo pads to your left! Roll up, roll up! Suddenly Rufus wanted to run at the couple and shout at them. But shout what? Fuck off? Leave us alone? What are you looking at? Or, possibly, I'm not like the others. Not me, I'm not one of them. He wasn't sure whom he hated most at that moment: Mr and Mrs Normal, or himself.

'Sit down, Rufus,' Belinda took his arm. 'We are going to play Chinese Whispers.'

He let himself be persuaded onto a corner of tartan rug. What was the point in denying it? He was one of them, after all. Hadn't he come on their bus? He belonged in the circus every bit as much as they did. He lay back and closed his eyes. Miraculously, the sun came out. Ten minutes later he risked taking off his jacket, settled himself more comfortably, and let the warm rays sooth his frazzled nerves, and lull him into gentle sleep.

'Rufus.'

It was Kate's voice that pulled him back to consciousness an hour later.

'Come on,' she said, 'we're being dragged off to look at the pier. Chuff knows why.'

He clambered to his feet, brushed sand from his trousers, and followed the others. The pier was a shock. It had, it transpired, only recently been damaged by fire. As they drew closer the results of the blaze became startlingly clear. The far end, what looked like several hundred feet of it, had been devoured by the inferno so that all that remained were twisted metal girders, melted by the heat into a knot of blackened agony on the sand. The group edged closer to the safety barriers. There was something unspeakably desolate about the charred skeleton of the structure, and the few blackened beams that lay on the muddy sand, slimy from weeks in the water, like so many giant sticks of sodden charcoal. The grisly nature of this destruction was made all the more noticeable when compared to the part of the pier that had been saved. The end nearest the town remained intact and functioning, as if it had nothing to do with the mangled ruins attached to it. Slot machines pinged and chirruped in the arcade. The smell of candy floss and hot dogs drifted down upon them. People trod the sturdy boards, trying their luck on the one-armed bandits, bashing gophers, or grabbing at soft toys with a crane. Small children rode on the little merry-go-round. Pensioners sat on benches eating fish and chips. All was fun and frivolity and stability. And yet, a few yards further on, all was very far from fun. It was death and danger. But everyone chose to ignore it.

Rufus noticed Belinda step forward towards the burnt debris, as if mesmerised by what she saw. Agency pulled her back.

'You can't go in there, Belinda,' she said.

Belinda was silent now. Gone was the prattling, the cheerful chattering, the I'm-fine-and-doing-very-well Belinda. She seemed suddenly stripped bare. Her vulnerable inner self exposed to the gritty air.

Someone suggested they buy ice creams and everyone drifted away from the wreckage and up onto the working bit of pier. Rufus hesitated. Teach appeared at his elbow.

'My word, have you seen those, Ruf? Let's take a closer look,' he said, before meandering off on increasingly unsteady legs.

Rufus followed, not caring where he was led, wanting only to get away from the pier.

The object of Teach's interest turned out to be an area given over to sand sculptures. The complexity and artistry of the constructions was quite astonishing. There was a full-sized Beetle car, a Koala up a gum tree, a bust of Beethoven and an even more impressive one of Marilyn Monroe, a giant lobster, a group of sea gulls, and a scale model of the Starship Enterprise.

'Remarkable!' Teach wandered between the exhibits. 'The level of skill. The detailed execution.' As he spoke he swung his arms expressively. Unfortunately, one of his precious plastic bags was of the bio-degradable variety and chose that moment to degrade. Its contents spewed out, landing among the sculptures like oversized confetti.

'Oi! Get that rubbish out of here, you idiot,' the exhibition attendant came scuttling out of his kiosk. 'Look what you're doing!'

'Sorry!' Teach staggered about trying to collect his things. '*Mea Culpa!* Not to worry. Soon have everything back in place.' He reached forward to pluck a polystyrene cup from Marilyn's cleavage. At that moment an exceptionally strong puff of wind caught him square between the shoulders and he toppled over, his landing softened by the starlet's biscuity bosom.

'You moron!' the attendant bellowed as Teach floundered like a marooned piece of sealife.

Rufus raised his eyes heavenwards. As he did so his vision swept past something odd in the distance. He refocused. It was Livingstone running. Running towards the slowly encroaching sea. Now Rufus saw that others were running too. Well Meaning, and Agency. Even Brian. Now they were all charging, as a herd, towards the water. And there was something in the flopping waves. No, not something. Someone. Rufus felt his throat constrict. Kate. Where was Kate? He scanned the figures but could not find her. Now he was running too. Tearing across the sand, his feet dragging in the grainy, uneven surface of the dried out beach. He tried to run faster but, as if he were in some terrible nightmare, the water receded before him. He gained ground only with the most momentous effort. Air rasped in and out of his lungs. He pushed himself harder, cursing his neglected, unathletic body. Now he could see panic-stricken faces. He could see mouths opening and shutting. He knew there must be noise and shouting and screaming, but he could hear nothing. Only the pounding of his own heart in his ears. Where was she? Where *was* she? Ahead of him Livingstone was kneeling in the soupy surf, grabbing at the woman's body as the tide bore it in. Rufus ploughed through the water and fell beside him. As he did so he caught sight, at last, of Kate, standing with the others, her face ashen, her expression one of shock. She was there. She was alive. She was OK. He felt his breath beginning to steady. He looked down at the figure in front of him. Well Meaning helped Livingstone to turn her over. Belinda. Her hair, for once, was not a shapeless fluffiness, but a seal-slick brown cap. The sea had washed away her make-up and her face looked surprisingly youthful and fresh.

Rufus thought he could see in her now, in this moment of her death, how she must have been as a young girl, and how she might have been through life, had she not been dealt the hand of cards that were given her. Well Meaning's tears splashed saltily into the salty sea.

Rufus became aware of an eerie, haunting, almost unearthly noise. It was a thin keening, a high wail of pain, that cut through his mind and imprinted itself indelibly onto his memory. Mute Mavis had found her voice.

CHAPTER SEVEN

The morning of his interview saw Rufus blundering about his flat in a frantic attempt to be on time. He felt as if the hands of his watch were whirring round at three times their normal speed, while his own actions were slowed to a leaden-limbed crawl. He had endured another fitful, sweaty night, and his hands trembled as he tried to knot his tie. An unpleasant metallic taste had taken up residence in his mouth. The telephone rang.

'Haven't you left yet?' his mother wasted no time on pleasantries.

'Clearly not. And good morning to you too.'

'You don't want to be late for the interview.'

'Which is why I haven't time to talk right now. How did you know about it, anyway?'

'Matthew spilled the beans. You are going to wear a tie, aren't you? And a jacket?'

'I'm a lunatic, Mummy, not an imbecile, remember?' There was a pause at the other end of the line. Rufus wedged the receiver between shoulder and ear and shrugged on his jacket. 'Anything else you wanted to check? Trousers? Head, perhaps?'

'Don't try to be clever in the interview, Rufus. People don't like it.'

'I'll fight my natural urge to shine. Now, I really must go.'

'Yes. Well... good luck, darling.'

Rufus was stunned. Words of affection from his mother were so rare as to be collector's items, and yet here she was, not two days after their latest set to, wishing him luck and calling him... it was astounding. Had he finally found something he could do that would meet with her approval?

'Thanks. Thank you, Mummy,' he said. He put down the phone, eyebrows raised, allowing himself a small smile.

The building that was home to the Herefordshire Herald was brown and drab on the outside, and magnolia and drab on the inside. Rufus fidgeted in the foyer as the receptionist checked her log for his name.

'You can go in,' she said without bothering to look up. 'Through there. Second door on the left.'

'Thank you so much,' Rufus gushed, smiling hard. He knew he was over compensating. He was aware that his appearance was beginning to give away his fragile state. He must not submit to panic. He must not. He must smile. Affect a breezy, happy-go-lucky tone. Enthuse. That was the secret. At all costs, deflect attention from the sweatiness of his brow, or the pastiness of his skin, or the alarming shaking of his hands if they were left unchecked.

He pushed through the fire door and made his way down the narrow corridor. The carpet boasted a jagged geometric pattern which made him feel dizzy. He raised his chin slightly and tried hard not to look down. A young woman squeezed past him, frowning at his rather superior pose. Second door on the left bore the inscription in plastic 'James Renfrew,

HR'. In his befuddled state this seemed to Rufus to suggest something vaguely royal. He knocked.

Inside the room sat the distinctly unregal Mr Renfrew. Beside him was a plump, middle-aged lady with a fondness for pink, which did her no favours whatsoever.

Mr Renfrew raised his backside out of his chair a few inches and extended a pudgy paw. 'Ah, Rufus Waters? Good, good. Take a seat,' he said, having given Rufus a disturbingly feminine handshake. 'This is Mrs Evans, head of our sales department. The successful candidate for this position will be working directly under her,' he added, without the merest hint of humour.

'Wonderful!' cried Rufus, perching on the red plastic chair which had been placed in the centre of the room, just a little too far from the interviewers. As if familiarity was being discouraged from the start. Rufus leaned forward, smiling, resisting the urge to wipe his forehead with the back of his sleeve. His mouth felt so dry he feared it would soon make his voice horribly husky. Not good for someone wanting to work in Telesales. To steady his hands he placed them firmly on his lap, fingers laced.

'So, Rufus,' Mr Renfrew picked up a pencil and held it, poised for action, above his notepad, 'what makes you think you are the man for the job?'

'Well, I'm hard-working,' Rufus offered, 'and reliable.'

Mrs Evans pursed her lips. 'But you've never sold advertising space before,' she said.

'No.'

'There is a level of skill involved, you know,' she told him.

'I'm sure,' said Rufus. 'I'm a quick learner. And keen to take on a new challenge. I think sales, working for the Herald, well, it could be just the exciting sort of opening I'm looking for.' Even to him it sounded unconvincing. Nobody went into Telesales for a challenge, for heaven's sake. It was the job you did when you couldn't do anything else. When all other reasonable avenues of employment were closed to you. Locked, bolted, and barred.

Mr Renfrew cleared his throat. 'I have to say, you are a little... older than most of our sales team.' He picked up Rufus's application form and scanned it briefly. 'You're not working at present, I see?'

'No.'

'And there seem to be some gaps in your work experience.'

Mrs Evans nodded, reading over his shoulder. 'Quite long gaps. Why is that?'

Mr Renfrew and Mrs Evans looked up at Rufus, faces expectant, waiting for an explanation they could content themselves with. Rufus hesitated. He had seen those expressions before. He had sat on just such a chair in just such an interview more times than he cared to count, and always came this crucial moment. Those expectant faces. Explain yourself, they said. Convince us. Give us something to write in this little box and we can give you this ridiculously unimportant job and then we can all get on with our lives.

Rufus remembered being nineteen. The chair had been blue and the interviewers both women, but the expressions had been the same. Then, too young to know any better, he had tried honesty.

'I've spent some time in hospital,' he had told them.

The women had leaned forward, arranging their features to show kindly concern.

'The Belmont Hospital,' he had added.

The women, as one, recoiled, their faces closed.

On the second occasion he had been a year older and just as clueless, still clinging to the belief that the truth could set you free. This time there were three on the panel, all men.

'I've had some mental health issues in the past. But I'm receiving treatment now and...' His voice had trailed off as the interviewers silently shut their files and began to study the floor.

Another time Rufus had sought to reassure his smiling prospective employers.

'It's not really a problem at all. I mean, the medication these days is extremely effective. And I've got an excellent psychiatrist. Dr Spinks, you may have heard of him?'

There had been much fidgeting and clearing of throats, amongst which someone had mumbled the words, 'We'll let you know.'

Rufus already knew. He knew that no one wanted to take on a problem employee. He knew that no one wanted to risk embarrassing, or possibly even dangerous, antics in the workplace. He knew that no one wanted to give a job to a nutter. After all, why would they? Hard enough to get a good day's work out of a so-called normal person; what chance with some loon who might start raving at any moment, for all they knew? And even if said nutcase did manage to confine his more unacceptable behaviour to his own home, how many sick days would that add up to in any given financial year? Why take the risk?

Rufus took a deep breath, licked his dry lips, and put the second phase of his Master Plan into action. Tell Lots Of Lies.

'Ah yes, I can explain that. You see, I am a writer.'

Mr Renfrew and Mrs Evans reacted with mild interest.

Rufus ploughed on. 'Yes. So I've spent a great deal of time doing research for my book. Abroad. It's about... Africa.'

'A novel?' Mr Renfrew wanted to know.

'That's right. A long one.'

'A saga?' Mrs Evans was visibly softening. 'I do enjoy a good saga.'

'Definitely a saga. Heaps happening. Cast of thousands. Exotic locations. Wild animals. Heat and passion. That sort of thing.'

'Well,' Mr Renfrew smiled, 'naturally here at the Herald we pride ourselves on the quality of our journalists. Perhaps you have ambitions to move up the ladder from Telesales, eh? Work your way to, who knows, junior reporter. After an appropriate amount of time, of course.'

Mrs Evans shook her head. 'There's plenty of room for Mr Waters' creative talents in Sales, Mr Renfrew.'

'Just so,' nodded Mr Renfrew, 'I only meant that Mr Waters might consider the broader possibilities available to him by joining the Herald, given his abilities.'

Amazing. Seconds ago they had been regarding Rufus as a work shy, middle-aged failure. Now they were fighting over him and calling him Mr Waters. There was clearly something in this lying business. It was a strategy he decided then and there to use more often.

Ten minutes later, hands had been shaken, forms had been signed, and Rufus had got himself his first job in ten years. He left the room with as much composure as he could muster, fighting the desire to run. Once outside he hastened to the nearest dark alley, scuttled down it, and was copiously, noisily, and abundantly sick.

That night he decided to celebrate. Not The Grapes. He

needed a new venue. Somewhere that would reflect his status as a Bloke With A Job. Somewhere hip and happening. After roaming the streets for over an hour, his hair dampened by the drizzle that had replaced the sunshine of the previous weekend, he came across a throbbing nightclub. The enormous, pulsating neon sign above the door read 'Havit!'. A large man in black, wearing dark glasses, presumably against the glare of the strobing lettering, stood, arms folded, guarding the entrance. He stared blankly at Rufus through mirrored lenses and then stepped aside. Rufus took this as a sign that he was considered suitable. His new identity must be taking shape nicely. Already doors were, quite literally, opening. He braced himself and went inside. Nothing could have prepared him for the ghastliness of the music. On the street all he could hear was the thudding bass. Once down the treacherously dark stairs and into the club proper the cacophony was revealed in all its hideousness. Discordant melodies collided with one another beneath the high whine of a synthesised noise that seemed to come from another piece of music entirely. The relentless rhythm was bashed out, apparently, by a hundred hungry savages beating war drums. For a second Rufus's resolve weakened. How could anyone who truly loved and understood music tolerate this? All he wanted to do was flee. Run back up the stairs, into the cool night air, and get himself to The Grapes and a decent pint. But no. No. This was an important part of what he had set out to do. He must be strong. Alcohol might help. He pushed his way through the twitching crowd around the dance floor and, not without difficulty, located the bar. He squeezed into a non-existent gap in the revellers and signalled to the barman.

'What'll it be?'

Rufus squinted into the gloom, trying to identify the labels on the rows of bottles. He looked up and down the black shiny bar. 'Haven't you any beer?' he asked, noticing the absence of taps.

'We've got Buds,' the barman inclined his head at the bottles on the shelves.

Rufus grimaced. 'What's popular in here?' he yelled above the din.

The barman shrugged. 'Breezers. Ice-ups. Frootz. Depends what you like.'

'Something to wake me up.'

'Vodka and Red Bull,' the barman seemed certain. 'Keep you going all night.

Rufus watched him mix the fizzing drink. Even in the flashing lights and intermittent blackness he could see it was a worrying pink colour. He took a sip.

'Jesus! It tastes like bubble gum and paint stripper.'

'Does the business though,' the barman took his money with a grin. 'You'll see.'

Rufus forced down more of the revolting concoction and turned to watch his fellow clubbers. It did not take him long to realise that he was easily a decade older than most of them. He risked a casual smile in the direction of two girls near the bar. They regarded him blankly and then looked away. It was hard to know what to do next. Even if he did find someone to talk to, conversation would have been nigh on impossible without the use of megaphones. And there was no way he was going to set foot on the dance floor. He valued his limbs too much. He downed the rest of his toxic drink and nodded to the barman for a refill. The second glass didn't taste quite so frightful. By his third he had almost convinced himself he was beginning to get used to the flavour. By the fourth he was stupidly drunk and urgently in need of the loo.

'I need a piss,' he bellowed at the barman.

'Bogs are over there.'

Rufus picked his way cautiously, and more than a little unsteadily, towards the far end of the room. He passed a noisy table of women who were clearly celebrating a hen night. The girl seated in the corner caught his eye. It was a fleeting connection, but Rufus noticed it. She was pretty, in a fresh-faced, no make-up sort of way. Lots of silky blonde hair and nice teeth. Rufus paused. They were just exchanging faltering smiles when he was knocked off his feet by a particularly large silverback gorilla.

Rufus cried out as he was pinned to the floor by the massive creature that had fallen on top of him, but his voice was lost amidst the fur. It was only as the animal was hauled to its feet that he saw it was an idiot in a horribly authentic costume. The image flashed through Rufus's head of a flayed ape, its skin donated to the noble cause of Stripograms. He shut his eyes against it and staggered to his feet. His head had connected with the floor with some force and now ached badly. He rubbed it clumsily.

'Sorry, mate!' shouted the gorilla. 'Can't see fuck-all in this get up!'

Rufus was about to remonstrate but caught sight of the attractive blonde hurrying towards him. He stayed silent – appearing cool while arguing with an oversized monkey would be tricky to pull off.

'Are you OK?' the girl asked. 'You hit your head when you fell.'

'Sorry? Can't hear you.'

'Your head!' she repeated, gesturing. 'Come with me.'

She led him through a door and across a hallway. A second door opened into an entirely different world. An oasis of calm and comfort. Here were soft lights, squidgy sofas, fluffy rugs, and gently flowing lava lamps. Rufus saw that the bar continued in a circle, so that clubbers could access alcohol while they slumped. The girl helped him to a well-padded bar stool and placed a cool hand on his temple.

'Are you sure you're not hurt? You can't be too careful with head injuries.'

'No, really. I'm fine. Thank you for caring.' He smiled at her. 'This is much better. In here, I mean. Away from that racket.'

The girl laughed. 'This is the chilling room,' she said.

'Clearly it pays to know these things. I'm afraid I'm a bit of a novice at this. At this sort of place.'

'Me too. I'm only here because of my cousin's hen night. I'm Abigail, by the way,' she held out a hand.

Rufus took it and on impulse, instead of giving it a formal shake, put it to his lips for a kiss. His amazement at his own action was surpassed only by the amazement he felt when Abigail blushed and smiled at him. He made a mental note to get in a supply of Red Bull and vodka at home. 'I'm Rufus,' he told her. 'Will you let me buy you a drink?'

'Oh, yes. Thank you. I'll have a pineapple juice, please.'

'Really? You sure? I couldn't face this place without large quantities of alcohol.'

'I don't drink very often. I've already had some of Cindy's champagne. What are you having?'

Rufus hesitated. 'Actually, I think I'll join you in a fruit juice.' He summoned the barman and ordered the drinks, leaning close to instruct him to put another shot of vodka in his. He now remembered that he had been on his way to the gents. An urgent need began to make itself felt. He knew he should go, but did not want to break the spell of the moment. Here he was actually chatting up a gorgeous young woman. No, sod it, *being* chatted up. How often did that happen? He couldn't risk her attention slipping, or one of her cackling friends appearing to whisk her away. He would just have to think about something else. There was no time to lose.

Spurred on by a dangerous combination of vodka, caffeine, nerves, and a painful bladder, Rufus went for the direct approach. 'So, some lucky boyfriend waiting to meet up with you later, perhaps?' he asked.

Abigail shook her head. 'No. I was living with someone, but it didn't work out. We split up a while ago. Still friends, though. How about you?'

'Me? Oh, no. Nobody. No partner. Free as a bird.' A very fuzzy-headed and pretty darn wobbly bird at that.

'Really? I was sure you'd have a glamorous girlfriend in tow.' Abigail looked at him, clearly waiting for more detail.

Rufus experienced a painful flashback. Another bar. Another girl. Another hopeful face regarding him with just that blend of interest and wariness. Another prospective girlfriend daring him to disappoint her. He saw his younger self sitting opposite, trying to explain.

'You see, I have this illness. Nothing catching, don't worry, nothing like that. It just makes it difficult for me to get to know people. For people to get to know me... sometimes I need to spend a few weeks in hospital.'

'Oh, you poor thing,' Prospective Girlfriend had reached out to him.

'The Belmont Hospital.'

Prospective Girlfriend had slowly withdrawn her hand.

Rufus closed his eyes, rubbing them, trying to stay focused, but further memories assailed him. The girl with the rust red hair and long legs. A French bistro. Same expression. Himself blundering again.

'I have a fantastic psychiatrist. You'd love him, really. He's happy to do couple therapy too....'

Rust Red had laughed nervously and then studied her fingernails.

And the one with the bedroom eyes and the full bosom. Oh God, she had been beautiful. Even now he lusted after her, all these years later. His candour had been no more successful that time either.

'And of course a good mental hospital is just like The Priory only cheaper!' he had assured her. 'The detox programme is terrific. I always come out feeling like a million dollars. Wheatgrass smoothies? Can't get enough of 'em.'

Bedroom Eyes had hissed at the barmaid to call her a cab.

Rufus couldn't let it happen again. He couldn't. Not now. Not with the New Improved Rufus Waters in town. Things were going to be different this time.

'No,' he leaned one elbow on the bar trying to effect nonchalance but in truth to stop himself sliding off his strangely swaying stool, 'you see, I'm a writer. I've spent a great deal of time abroad, researching my book. There really hasn't been time for a serious relationship.'

'Oh, wow. That sounds very dedicated. Very single-minded.'

Rufus sighed and nodded. 'I have had to make sacrifices.'

'For your art.'

'That's right. But, happily, I'm back for a while now.'

'No more travelling?'

'Not for the foreseeable. Have to get down to writing the thing now, you know. Still, I shall miss Africa.'

'Africa. Gosh, that must have been amazing. I have always wanted to travel through Africa.'

Rufus could smell victory. He could taste it. He could also feel his plumbing beginning to give way. He would have to cut to the chase. 'It is a magical place,' he agreed. 'Look, it's not easy to talk here, and it's getting late. I don't suppose you'd like to have dinner with me one night? I could tell you all about it.'

'OK,' she said. 'I think I'd really like that.'

With unseemly haste Rufus took her phone number and made his excuses. They were saying their goodbyes in the hallway, Rufus's eye firmly on the sign above the door of the gents, when Abigail recognised a song she liked being played.

'Oh! This is great. I actually know this one. Come on, let's dance!'

Before he could do anything about it, she had grabbed his hand and dragged him through the door and onto the dance floor. Rufus struggled to quell rising panic. Now she would find him out for certain. There was no way he could execute the smooth moves and frenzied gyrations of the other clubbers. But there was no escape. He couldn't fail now. He had secured both a job and a date in the same momentous day. He was king of the world! Sod it, shit or bust!

'OK, yeah!' he cried. 'Let's show these youngsters how it's done!' With a whoop he threw his hands above his head and went for it. Somewhere in the back of his mind he recalled a little poem Kate was fond of. Something about dancing like no one was watching. Clinging to this thought, and muscles clenched against possible urinary disaster, Rufus leapt and twirled and stomped and did, indeed, dance in a way that had, until that point, only ever been witnessed by the uncritical gaze of a small, stuffed, red squirrel.

CHAPTER EIGHT

The house Kate shared with her parents was modest, friendly, and unremarkable. It stood at the end of a narrow cul de sac on the Whitefields estate, which was made up of just eight such houses and four bungalows. The red brick and double glazed windows still looked as new, and the small patch of grass to the front was lovingly mowed and trimmed by her father every Sunday. Mam was in charge of hanging baskets and window boxes, and the flower beds in the back garden. Dad only did lawns. Kate hated the house and felt a nagging guilt for having such dark feelings towards it. There was nothing in the way it looked to object to. And inside the boxy rooms managed to be both light and cosy. The estate was peaceful and only a short bus ride from the city centre. No, there was nothing about the house itself to make any sensible person hate it. But then, Kate would never have described herself as a sensible person. And she had her own reasons for wishing the place would drop into a chasm brought about by a handy freak earthquake, or be beamed up by a passing alien space ship, or just get itself gone in any way it liked. For this was the house her parents had bought after Kate's first stay in a mental institution. This was the house they had moved to because they were so embarrassed, so ashamed (though of course they would never say such a thing), so mortified by their daughter's nutty behaviour that they had not been able to stay in Pontefract. This was the house they had run away to, to avoid all those pursed lips and tutting tongues and shaking heads. This was the house they had come to for an exciting new life in lovely Herefordshire, when really they all knew (though of course they would never say such a thing) that this was as far away from anyone who knew them as they could get where Kate's dad could find a job. This was the house where they had all convinced themselves, for a whole five chuffing minutes, that everything would be all right. But this was the house which had had its front door broken down twice already by the police. This was the house where Kate had been dragged screaming down the drive into the waiting ambulance. This was the house where her mam had stood on the tiny patch of tidy lawn and watered the grass with her tears as her only child was carted off to the loonie bin in full view of her lovely, new, friendly neighbours. This was the house that had had its garage door spray painted with the oh-so-friendly words 'Fucking Nutter Go Home.' Well, fuck *them*.

Kate sat at the kitchen table letting her mam pile toast in front of her. At the height of Kate's mania, her mother would enter a frenzy of cooking, as if she could cure her daughter by strength of will and home-cooked food alone.

Let me fix you a bit o' tea. 'Ow about a nice drop o' soup? I've just gorra cake out o' oven, sit yersen down and I'll fetch it over. Steak sarnie? Got to keep your strength up, Our Katie.

It was a wonder Kate wasn't a waddling size twenty by now. Her dad put on weight every time. Well, neither of them could abide waste. He had already left for his job at the fuel depot, a hearty bit o' scran in his tuck bag. Driving a petrol tanker could take it out of a person.

'D'you want an egg to go wi' that?' her mother asked.

Kate shook her head, 'Toast'll do me, Mam. Don't want to be late for rehearsal.' She patted the piece of sheet music beside her plate. 'First run through of my solo today.'

'Oh, aye? What you doing this time?' Her mam joined her at the table. She was nearly sixty, but her natural curls were still full and bouncy, even if they were more grey than brown now. 'Is it the one wi' all them high twiddly notes and a lot o' violins? Yer dad loves that'n.'

'No. That's Mozart, Mam. This is Purcell. *Dido's Lament.'*

A shadow passed over her mother's face. 'In't that the one you sang before, you know... in London?'

'Mam...'

'Don't go getting yoursen all worked up again, now, will you?'

'Mam, stop fussing. I'm fine. I can't wait to get started. I'm going to show all those snooty chuffing pearl-wearers what singing's all about. You just see if I don't.' She tried to sound as casual as she could, but it was hard not to let her excitement show. Dido's Lament. *The* most beautiful aria she had ever sung. The most gorgeous, most haunting, most sublime piece of music ever written. And yes, it had been what she was singing when she had lost it in London. How could she forget? How could any of them? 'I'll be all right, Mam,' she said.

'Aye, well. Just think on. Nowt's worth getting yoursen in a state over. Not even your music.'

But it was worth it – that was the whole buggering point. That was the thing her mam would never in a million years understand. Music was worth any price she had to pay. What was the alternative? How could she not sing? Might as well ask her not to breathe. Didn't they see that this was all she had left? This was the deal she had struck with the cruel fucking bastard of a god who had given her the blessing of this voice and the curse of this head. She would sing. She would sing in the cathedral in front of a whole bunch of people. And if doing that send her stark raving chuffing bonkers, then it did, and they would all just have to live with it. She would have to live with it. Because she would, beyond the smallest buggering doubt, die without it.

The rehearsal was joyous. Kate could feel her soul and her mind energised by the music, lifted and healed by each perfect note as she sang them. When the session came to an end she gathered up her things. A small movement from behind a pillar caught her attention. Teach emerged shyly from the shadows and wandered towards her.

'Teach? What are you doing lurking in dusty corners?'

'Was I lurking? Sorry. Didn't realise.'

'Well, what did you think?'

'Of the dusty corners?'

'Of the singing. I thought it went pretty bloody well, if I do say so myself.'

'Oh yes. Excellent, Kate. Quite wonderful, in fact.'

'Of course, the choir's a man light. No Rufus. Again. Typical of him. He decides he wants to change his life, and that's that. He doesn't give a toss about anyone else. How flaky is that?' She looked at Teach closely for a moment. He seemed subtly changed somehow. She frowned. 'So, any sign of those test results yet?' she asked.

'Oh, yes, as a matter of fact. Got them earlier today.'

'And?'

Teach hesitated, seeming to search for words. On another day, when Kate might not have been so taken up with her music, her head not quite so full of crotchets and semi breves and minims and quavers, she might have thought this strange. Might have acknowledged that, for all Teach's muddled mind, for all that he often selected a startling alternative to the word he was after, he was never stuck for something to say.

The pause continued, and then at last he said quietly, 'All pretty much as I had anticipated. No real surprises.'

'You'll be around to blag pints off the rest of us for a while yet, then?'

'*Deo Volente.*'

'What's that?'

Teach breathed deeply, pulling back his shoulders, straightening up, as if marshalling himself for some great effort. 'Absolutely,' he said with a grin. 'Years of scrounging ahead. I plan to cost you all a small fortune.'

'In that case, I'll take you to The Grapes, so you can listen to me whine on some more about Rufus.' She began to make her way to the door.

Teach followed. '*Quidquid excusatio prandium pro*, I always say.'

'Which to we poorly educated plebs is?'

'Any excuse for lunch.'

CHAPTER NINE

Rufus stood beside Mrs Evans and tried not to look as ill as he felt. The wretched woman was in a particularly sickly shade of pink, which was provoking to critical levels the nausea that threatened to be his undoing. Where had she found such a shade? What could it be called? Sugar pink, perhaps, like those revolting mice he had eaten as a child? No, that wasn't it. Nipple pink, he decided, and quelled a shudder. On his first day at work he did not want to be entertaining thoughts of his boss's body parts.

'This is your workstation,' she told him, pointing unnecessarily at the cramped peg-boarded cubicle in front of them.

There was a desk, a phone, an uncomfortable looking chair, and a pile of telephone directories. The gloomy walls of the little booth were studded with drawing pins and torn corners of missing memos. An inappropriately colourful postcard of the Seychelles hung limply in the top left hand corner, no doubt left behind by the previous inhabitant. Rufus wondered what had happened to them. Had they moved on to bigger and better things? Or was the picture of palm trees and turquoise seas the final blow, the thing that sent them screaming out of the building? He could imagine the environment driving people mad. Perhaps it would be an advantage to be ahead of the others in this respect. He shook the thought away, reminding himself this was the New Improved Rufus Waters. No trace of nuttiness could remain. He forced himself to focus on what Mrs Evans was telling him.

'It's up to you to keep it tidy. No sticky tape on the pegboards – when it's removed the surface comes with it. You will be supplied with drawing pins. We discourage hot drinks at your desk, but water is allowed. Eating is not. You know where the coffee room is. Here are your induction papers. Nothing complicated. Just read through and sign here, here, and here. I'll send Sarah over a minute to show you how to use the phone. Here's a copy of this week's script. Here's a list of our rates. You'll need one of these,' she pressed a calculator into his sweaty hand. 'You can borrow one for now. You'll be expected to get your own by the end of the week. That's a summary of offers and specials for next week. You've had your run through, so you know what it's all about. Any questions, I'm in the office over there. Best way to learn is just to get on with it. Important thing is your tone of voice. And don't lose your temper, no matter how much you feel like it. They are allowed to be rude and foul-mouthed – we are not. How is the book coming along?'

Momentarily thrown by the question, Rufus recovered himself quickly, 'Oh, very well, thank you.'

Mrs Evans treated him to a rare and strangely unnerving smile, and then strode away on kitten heels. Rufus tested out his chair, fiddling with the height adjustment, wincing when it elevated him suddenly and trapped his knees under the cheap surface of the desk. He leaned back to peer around the walls of his cubbyhole at his co-workers. There were eight other workstations, all occupied by what appeared to be teenagers. There were two men, though it was doubtful they qualified for the name. One sported the most impressive bout of acne Rufus had seen since he left school. The other had ginger hair cut, apparently, to make him resemble a muppet. The rest of the positions were taken up by off-the-peg girls. He doubted he could have told them apart if required to. They were all dressed as if on their way to a lunch party in a wine bar, or in a couple of cases, a hen party somewhere noisier. Necklines plunged and hemlines soared. In between was a lot of polyester and acrylic. There was clearly a competition going on to see who could outdo whom on the make-up front. Hairdos were another unifying factor. Most had long, centre parted, ironed hair, although there was one with gelled shagginess and an asymmetrical fringe thing going on. The girl nearest him was chewing gum so loudly he could hear it above the murmur of the sales patter that filled the room like a Buddhist chant. He picked up the papers and did his utmost to make sense of them. The idea that there was actually a script to work from appalled him. He wasn't an actor. He hadn't expected to have to give some sort of performance. The thought of it was ghastly. He was here to sell a bit of space on the local rag. Why make it more complicated than it was? You choose your potential advertiser from one of the directories, or a rival paper, he had been told. You phone them up and try to persuade them to book up a series of ads. You fill it all in on the form provided, put it into a pile, and hand the lot in at the end of the day.

He rubbed his eyes. His mouth felt drought dry, and a sharp headache had set itself up behind his eyebrows. He tried not to think about how much he missed his medication. He had always known the first few days would be rough. It was just a matter of toughing it out. Of being determined. Of not letting the demon panic take possession of his psyche. Distraction, that was the key. He must keep busy at all costs. He narrowed his eyes at the lineage rates, reminding himself how a successful sale depended on getting the customer to upgrade to a box display. Or was it a display box? He picked up the phone and listened to it buzz. It already felt heavy in his hand. Why couldn't they have those natty little head microphones he'd seen on TV commercials? There was a certain appeal to one of those. A little media-savvy. A smidge cutting edge. But no. Ugly plastic phones for all.

Suddenly Rufus felt a swirling dizziness. He gripped the desk and waited for it to pass, but it got worse. Soon the holes in the pegboard were hopping about before him. His mouth began to run with salt, his stomach tighten. He swallowed hard. Water might help. Or coffee. Yes, coffee with lots of sugar. He glanced about him. No sign of the promised Sarah to explain the mysterious complexities of the telephone system. He got up, his chair making an unhelpfully loud twanging noise as it was relieved of his weight. Muppet and Chewing Gum swivelled round to give him disapproving looks. He smiled wanly, mouthing apologies as he backed away towards the door.

The coffee room was not a place anyone would want to linger – a successful ploy on the part of the management. There was no heating, and the small window looked out onto the rear end of the bus depot. The sink harboured coffee-stained mugs and spilt sugar, despite the numerous notices demanding cleanliness and consideration for others. Rufus ran the tap and splashed his face with cold water. There were no paper towels, so he remained dripping as he rummaged through the cupboards. He found brandless coffee in a two-litre drum and an assortment of sweeteners, but no real sugar. He fell upon a squashed box of paracetamol tablets. OK, it was medication of sorts, but not what he was giving up. Normal people took paracetamol. Normal people with normal headaches. He swallowed two quickly, hearing the door open behind him as he did so. It was Fringe and Muppet.

Rufus nodded at them and stood aside to let the boy organise their drinks. Nobody spoke. Muppet put dusty coffee powder into mugs, sniffing loudly as he did so. Fringe leaned back against the wall, arms folded, looking at Rufus with undisguised animosity. He feigned interest in something through the window, though it was hard to be convincing. Brick walls and parked buses presented very little by way of spectacle. He felt the girl's eyes upon him. Felt her taking in his tremors, his perspiration, his general state of debilitation. Why couldn't she leave him alone? Why couldn't she talk to Muppet about the weekend, or celebrities, or alcohol, or shagging, or whatever it was the youth were supposed to be bothered about these days? The more the silence grew, the worse he felt. Swallowing became difficult. He was aware of his heart rate increasing. No, mustn't let it do that. Steady, now. But there, his breathing was becoming more rapid too. And shallower, restricted by a tightening in his chest. Oh God, not now. Not here! He dug his nails into his palms, frantically trying to divert his sub-conscious from imagined threat to manageable, real pain. It didn't work. Adrenalin flooded his circulatory system. His mind screamed at him, *Run, run! Run, you idiot. Flee, now, before it's too late!* He rubbed his temples and fought to steady his breathing, but it was hopeless. Air rasped in and out of his lungs as if he were in the throes of an asthma attack. He knew in a few seconds he would be clawing the suffocating air. He had to get out. *Run, run, you stupid bastard, run!*

'No! I won't!' he said aloud.

Muppet stopped stirring the coffee. Fringe straightened up, peering warily at Rufus. The stuffy little room was filled with the smell of his panic. He dived at the sink and splashed his face once more, turning to face the others, water dripping from his nose and chin. They continued to regard him wordlessly.

'Hot,' he gasped, 'just a little hot. In here. Isn't it? Does… the window… open? No. No.' He struggled with the locked latch. It was all his claustrophobic inner-child needed for the screaming ab-dabs to take hold. Barging past his gawping colleagues he gave in to his by now hysterical sub-conscious and fled.

CHAPTER TEN

Two nights later Rufus sat across the table from Abigail, a sizzling platter between them. The Thai restaurant had been his idea. It was familiar ground for him, though he had never taken a girl there before. The waiters were smiling at him even more than usual, clearly surprised and amused by the fact that he was so obviously, he felt sure, on a first date. Ordinarily he found the food at The Golden Noodle irresistible. Tonight, however, the first whiff of Nam Prik threatened to be his undoing. He had been fighting nausea for days now, and it took all his energy not to run gagging for the door. He was aware of sweat beginning to bead his brow once more and what he knew to be an unattractive pinkness flushing his face. Abigail looked a picture of coolness and composure. Gentle Thai music plinked and plonked in the background. The murmured conversation of their fellow diners provided a soft bass hum. Rufus put on his brightest smile.

'So, Abigail, tell me all about yourself,' he said as they began to eat.

'Oh, there's not much to tell, really. I'm living with my parents again at the moment. And I work at Take A Hike.'

'The shop with all the climbing gear and walking stuff?'

'That's the one. Not much of a job, to be honest, but I do get a good discount.'

'You're into all that then, are you? Climbing, hiking.... you do look very fit.'

Abigail smiled. 'I'm afraid I'm a bit of an anorak when it comes to outdoor pursuits.'

Rufus laughed, a smidge too loudly. 'Anorak! That's very good. Oh shit!' he added as he knocked over his glass of water, swamping the table. He dabbed at the flood frantically with his napkin. 'Bugger it! Sorry. I'm a clumsy idiot.' He succeeded only in creating more mess by trailing his napkin though a dish of green curry sauce, spreading stickiness everywhere.

Abigail came to his rescue. 'Here, let me,' she said. She used her own napkin and quickly restored order.

There was an awkward little silence. Rufus fought to steady his shaking hands. He abandoned his chopsticks and grabbed a fork, aware that Abigail was watching him closely.

'Are you feeling OK?' she asked.

'Yes fine, thank you. Completely fine.'

'Only, I noticed your hands are shaking, and you do look a bit hot. Perhaps you're coming down with flu or something.'

'My hands? Oh, no, take no notice. It's just malaria.'

'What?!'

'Nothing to worry about. A legacy from my time in Africa. Plays up a bit sometimes, that's all.'

'You poor thing.'

'I don't like to make a fuss. Sorry if it bothers you.'

'Oh no, of course not. Please, don't think that. Is there anything I can do?'

'There's nothing. I'm used to it. It will pass in a few days.

Let's just enjoy our meal.' Rufus mustered a heroic little smile.

Abigail leaned forwards and put her hand on his. 'I think you're very brave,' she told him.

Rufus's smile broadened. 'How about a drop of wine?'

'OK. Why not? And you can tell me more about Africa and all about this wonderful book you're writing.'

And Rufus did just that. Having had time to read up on the Dark Continent, he was able to regale Abigail with tales of his journeys along the Namibian Skeleton Coast, his trek up Mount Kilimanjaro, his trip by canoe down the Limpopo, and other choice excerpts from the Imaginary Travels of the New Improved Rufus Waters. He added some details about the book itself, and watched as the poor girl's defences crumbled before his slightly blurry eyes.

An hour later they left The Golden Noodle arm in arm. It was a damp night, but not actually raining, and Rufus quickly found himself enjoying the novelty of strolling through the city, part of a pair, a man and his woman out for the night. All wonderfully sane and normal and pretty well devoid of nuttiness. Things were going well.

And then they reached the high town precinct.

A small crowd stood watching a commotion. Shouts and jeers could be heard.

'Oh,' Abigail stopped, 'what's happening there?'

As they looked on, the gathered throng parted to reveal Teach at its centre. He looked even more fragile than usual and was clearly distressed and more than a little drunk. Three long-limbed youths were baiting him, lobbing cruel comments and vicious jibes in his direction like so many rocks. Rufus could see they had emptied Teach's collecting bags onto the paving and were kicking the strewn contents about, laughing at his concern for such rubbish.

'Stop that!' Teach shouted. 'Those are my things! Philistines. *Pax! Pax!'*

The youth in the red hoodie snorted, 'He's off his fucking head!'

'Sad bastard,' the second boy sneered. 'What d'you want with all this crap anyway?'

Teach lurched and stumbled in an effort to salvage his gleanings, as bus tickets, lighters, broken watches and empty polystyrene coffee cups were scattered in all directions.

'Can't you see, you brutes?' he cried. 'These are the treasures of our age! The marks of man! The sum total of our existence is here, in that which we discard!'

The youngsters pressed in closer. Red Hoodie gave Teach a shove that sent him sprawling.

Rufus took a step forwards, then hesitated. He could see Teach was unhurt. He glanced at Abigail. There was an expression of such disgust on her face, but he could not be certain whom it was for. The crowd shuffled back a little, some drifting away, others suddenly finding urgent things to do elsewhere.

One of the youths was shouting again. 'You're a fucking nutter, mate! You want locking up, you do!'

On his knees, Teach gathered as much of his precious collection as he could. He turned his face up to the melting crowd. 'Be warned, all of you! The Barbarians are at the gates of Rome!'

Rufus was in turmoil. He knew he should go to Teach's aid. He wanted to help him, really he did. But then Abigail would find out they knew each other. That he was friends with the sort of person who raved in public and flailed about amid rubbish. Would she still want anything to do with him? It wasn't as if Teach were really in any danger; he was pretty sure of that.

The tallest of the louts was getting bored. 'Come on, let's split. This sad wanker's getting on my tits,' he said.

Red Hoodie agreed. 'Yeah, leave him with his crap.'

The gang lumbered off, and the remainder of the onlookers slunk away.

'It's all right. He's not hurt.' The words were out of Rufus's mouth before he could stop them. He put his arm around Abigail's shoulders and steered her away from the scene. 'Come on,' he said. 'Don't want you getting cold.'

As they turned, on the edge of his vision he saw Teach look up and spot him.

'My friend!' Teach called, still on his knees, 'Look what they have done.'

Rufus hurried on, ignoring Abigail's surprised expression at his sudden burst of speed. He could still hear Teach's voice.

'It's all up for the human race!' he shouted. 'There is no hope! The sins of the fathers... those young thugs are our future. *Quod avertat Deus!'*

Rufus had almost reached the safety of the narrow alley that led into Church Lane, but as they rounded the corner Teach tried again.

'Have you changed your name to Peter now, Rufus?' he yelled.

Abigail stopped. 'He knows your name?'

'What? No, can't do,' Rufus shook his head and scooted her along, keener than ever to get her out of range of Teach's wavering cries.

'I'm sure I heard him call your name.'

'I didn't hear it. You must be mistaken. Come on, it's starting to rain.'

By the time they arrived at Abigail's house it was indeed raining quite heavily. They ran inside, breathless and dripping. In the hallway Abigail stood close to him, smiling.

'My parents are away,' she said, 'and anyway, I don't think you should go back out there in that terrible weather.'

Rufus tried hard to focus. Here was a gorgeous young woman gazing up at him with what he was fairly certain was a come-hither glint in her pretty blue eyes, and he felt like death. His cold sweats were changing into hot sweats with such rapidity now that it was making him dizzy. His hands were not only shaky, but numb to the wrists. A needle-sharp headache had set itself up behind his eyes, and his Thai dinner was threatening to reappear. On top of everything else, he could still hear Teach's voice. He should have gone to him. Should have helped him. Sod it, what was a man supposed to do?

'Come on.' Abigail had given up waiting for him to make his move and was leading him by the clammy hand towards the stairs.

Her bedroom was cheery and pink and still home to an impressive collection of childhood teddies and all things fluffy. There were lots of photos of Abigail ski-hatted and booted, or dangling off the side of a mountain, or sharing a windswept group hug with other warmly-dressed hearty types. Rufus gazed about him, trying not to let the pinkness of his surroundings increase his queasiness. For some reason, he kept thinking of blancmange. Abigail lit scented candles, switched off the light, and then, to Rufus's amazement, proceeded to take off all her clothes and arrange herself temptingly on top of the daisy-printed quilt. After a second's stunned hesitation, Rufus began fumbling with his own buttons. As he battled with his flies and hopped about to remove his trousers, worrying memories started to surface. The first saw him aged nineteen, in the back of a rusting Ford Cortina, hungrily kissing a skinny girl with poker straight hair and a slight squint. The girl wriggled herself into position beneath him as he hastened to undo his jeans. Into his head came the mellifluous tones of Dr Spinks as he sought to enlighten him about the side effects of his antidepressant drugs.

'Modern medication is a wonderful thing, Rufus, but yes, it's true, there can be side effects. And, in a small number of cases, these may result in some sexual dysfunction.'

The skinny girl gazed up at young Rufus expectantly. All he could do was mumble an apology and rezip his trousers.

'You have to understand,' Dr Spinks's transatlantic drawl continued, 'that for these medicaments to do their work they must, by their very nature, influence a range of actions and impulses. They have to do this in order to make you feel better.'

Another cloudy vision drifted before Rufus. A chesty girl with buckteeth, his parents' sitting room, borrowed porn on the video player. The chest heaved enthusiastically. Rufus looked at first hopeful, then desperate, then crestfallen, then utterly defeated.

'Sadly,' Dr Spinks went on, 'some patients have reported this resulting in an inability to achieve or maintain an erection. A downside, if you will.'

Back in Abigail's bedroom Rufus rubbed his eyes and shook his head, but still the nightmare phantasmagoria of his past sexual failures played out in front of his mind's eye. The next woman was a good few years older. Rufus sported a daring goatee. This time they were in bed actually succeeding in having noisy, energetic sex.

Dr Spinks explained, 'Happily, for these people, there is a wide variety of medication they might like to try. Anecdotal evidence suggests that erectile problems do not occur whilst using these drugs.'

The older woman cried out in ecstasy. Rufus bonked on furiously.

'However, it may be that, for a proportion of patients availing themselves of this combination treatment, there might be some difficulty in reaching orgasm.'

The woman squealed and gasped her way through another climax. Rufus changed position and continued to pound away.

'Interestingly, the feedback from the wives and girlfriends of these same patients has been very positive,' said the good doctor.

The older woman slept peacefully while Rufus sat up in bed, awake but exhausted and terminally frustrated.

The sound of Abigail's voice brought him back to the present, forcing him to open his eyes. To his relief the spectres appeared to have gone.

'Wow!' said Abigail, eyes fixed on Rufus's crotch. 'No problems with malaria there, then!'

He grinned, whipped off his plaid boxers, and flung himself onto the bed. Nobody could have been more surprised than Rufus when he found him enjoying energetic, fun, uninhibited, and, crucially, totally satisfying sex.

'Yes!' he cried, finally sated and spent, 'Yes, yes, yes! Fuck you, Spinksy!' With that he collapsed into the flowery pillows, blissfully content.

As he fell into a gloriously happy sleep he heard Abigail's puzzled voice ask softly, 'Who's Spinksy?'

CHAPTER ELEVEN

The waiting area of the Whitecross Health Centre was at standing room only that Friday morning. Kate was forced to squeeze herself onto the end of a nylon-covered length of seating next to a woman who must have weighed more than twenty stone. She marvelled at what it might be like to be so vast. How did a person get like that? Wasn't there a point when she must have realised that whatever it was she was eating was going to make her end up the size of a small country? Perhaps she had a feeder at home. Kate had seen a TV programme about feeders. They just kept on pushing food in front of whomever it was they wanted to control. Made them fatter and fatter until they could hardly chuffing walk. Then they'd got them. Right there. Stuffed, in every buggering sense of the word. Kate reckoned her mam had feeder potential, given half a chance. The woman next to her started up a scary wheezing. Now Kate felt bad for thinking unkind things about her. Then she felt cross for being made to feel bad. She added the crossness to the grumpiness just being at the Health Centre always brought on. Especially when she was there for her quarterly check up and chat with her GP. Now she was properly pissed off.

She was tempted to tell the receptionist her appointment was not urgent. Give it to some poor chuffer else. One of the ones sneezing their disgusting colds all over the magazines, maybe. Kate had read something once, in one of those very magazines more than likely, about how viruses stick to the pages of a harmless looking copy of People's Friend, or Gardening Today, just waiting for some unsuspecting patient, bored out of their snot-ridden minds, to look for something to read. And then, that was it. You came in with bronchitis, gave it to someone else, and went out with gastro enteritis. Chuffing marvellous. No, there would be no snippets of celeb gossip for Kate from that toxic pile of Bugs R Us. No, ta very much. She glanced at the clock above the reception desk. Should have been seen ten minutes ago. Dr Gregory always ran late. She liked to tell herself it was because he cared. Because he would not rush the important business of doctor patient interaction. But she knew the truth was he was a bit of a faffer. Meant well, in an irritating sort of way, but faffed. Couldn't help himself. Fiddled with his computer, struggled with printing out scripts, looked things up all the time. Lost things. Dropped things. Generally muddled through. She wasn't surprised. She had seen the family photo on his desk: the five children under six. Two sets of twins – you'd think they'd have called it a day at that, but no. Weren't GPs supposed to know about contraception? Poor beggar always looked far worse than most of his patients.

The cheerful plink-plonk of the receptionist's intercom chimed into her thoughts. Her name was called and she went through the fire doors and into Dr Gregory's surgery.

'Ah, Kate. Come in, sit down, won't keep you a minute,' he continued to peer through wire-rimmed specs at the jittery monitor in front of him. 'Just need to... there. Think that's done it. Now,' he gave her a brief smile, his gaze still sliding back to the computer screen as he spoke, 'how are you today?'

As an opener, Kate thought this was pretty lame. Could he think of nothing else? Nothing more original? More chuffing subtle? How was she supposed to answer that? She could give him the reply he was hoping for. Fine, Dr Gregory, just fine. Taking my lovely medication. Job going well. Loving choir practice. Looking forward to our concert in an oh-so-calm and normal way. That's what he wanted to hear, after all. She could save them all a heap of bother, say the right thing, and he would nod and smile and give her another prescription and send her on her happy, oh-so-calm and normal way. Job done. Next! Or, she could give him the truth. Tell it like it was. Say that she wasn't sleeping more than five hours a night. Let him know that she felt her medication was taking the edge off her performance so she had cut it down. Just the teensiest, weensiest bit. She knew what she was about. No need for anyone to panic. She should chuffing know, after all. She'd been on the stuff for nearly eight years. Eight years of pressing the little magic pills out of their crackling blister packs every morning. Eight years of getting the bloody things stuck in her throat. Eight years of starting the day with chalky proof that she was a nutter. That her sanity depended on getting those lovely drugs down her neck. Or else. Oh aye, she knew what she was about. She knew exactly how much to cut down, how ever-so-carefully to lift that comfy blanket of lithium from her little brain. Just a smidge. Just to let her be a tiny bit more herself. For the performance. Oh sure, she could sing on the stuff. Had been doing for ages. But it wasn't the same. She always knew it could never be. It was the real

Kate who was the songbird. Not some wrapped up, dampened down version. She had to let herself out to sing properly. To sing her best. The real Kate did that. But, and here was the daft buggering truth of it, the real Kate wouldn't be given the liberty to sing anywhere outside a locked room on a side ward in the Belmont. So, she had to be careful. She had to appear normal. Super-normal, in fact. And normal to Doctor Gregory meant smiley and calm and being a good girl and taking all her medication exactly as she was supposed to.

'I'm fine, Doctor,' she said.

'Good, good,' he reached over and tapped on his keyboard. 'I see you're on your regular maintenance dose at the moment. Is that suiting you?' He squinted at the screen.

'Yes. It's just fine.'

'Good,' he read through her notes as they scrolled up before him, 'no problems for quite a while now. Excellent. Excellent. Still working at… where was it?'

'Quickshopper. Yes, still there. Couldn't be happier. Still stocking those lovely shelves.'

He glanced at her, and she realised she was overdoing it. He might be a sleep-deprived, harassed heap of a man, but he still had that chuffing doctor's radar. That thing that alerted them to any little signs of nuttiness.

'And how about your singing?' he asked. 'I enjoyed the concert last year very much. Must be about time for the next one?'

'End of this month. It's going to be a corker. You should definitely come. We're doing a bit of Handel, bit of Mozart, bit of gorgeous old Purcell. Tell all your friends. Tickets are selling out, you know.'

'Really? I wouldn't want to miss it. I'll start organising the babysitter.' He continued to look at her notes as he spoke. 'And you're not feeling under too much pressure? I know you put a lot into your singing. We don't want you overdoing things, now, do we?'

How she hated that 'we'. So patronising. So ridiculous. So chuffing untrue. How did he know what she wanted, for a start? Did he think she wanted to *under* do things? To half do them? To hold back out of fear? Fear of herself? Daft beggar. Didn't he see that this was the one thing in her whole sad life that made her feel alive? It might suit him to keep her dosed up with that poisonous crap, keep her quiet, keep her manageable. She couldn't live like that. She wouldn't live like that. Not when it came to her singing. She put on her brightest smile.

'Oh, don't you worry about me, Doctor. I'm looking after myself. Being sensible. Taking my medication, need it or not.'

Doctor Gregory's ears pricked up and paused in his keyboard tapping. He turned to look at her properly now. Kate continued to smile, but did not trust herself to speak further. The expression on his face told her she had already blown it. Shite!

Doctor Gregory smiled back at her. 'Glad to hear that, Kate. Why don't I just book you in for a quick blood test, eh? No harm in that, is there?'

'Oh, I wouldn't want to waste your time. Have you seen it out there this morning? Place is a sell out. Wouldn't want to take up a space with the nurse as well.'

'It's no trouble, really. You can come back on Monday, it'll be quieter then. Better to be on the safe side, don't you think?'

He carried on smiling, but he wasn't looking at her now; he was back at his keyboard, punching in with chewed fingers a time and a date for a test. A test that would reveal her lithium levels. A test that would show him she had been cutting back. A test that would lead to more tests, and more appointments, and on and on and on. Kate kept a hold on the panic that was rising up inside her. Super-normal. Super-chuffing-normal. She had to buy herself some time.

'Can't do Monday,' she said. 'Sorry. Mam's birthday. Taking her off for the day. Coach trip to the Costwolds. You know, picture postcard cottages, antique shops, cut-glass accents, whiff of royalty in the air. Can't do Monday.'

'OK. The phlebotomist is in on Thursday. We'll make it for then, shall we? Ten o'clock be alright?' He held her gaze, daring her to try to wriggle further.

'Oh, aye. Thursday at ten'll be just fine, Doctor.' Chuffing hell. Kate did a quick calculation in her head. Test on Thursday, results not back before the beginning of the week. Another few days to call her in to see him. She could be busy then. Put him off. Play for a few more days. Just a few more days. The smile on her face was beginning to stiffen.

Doctor Gregory wasn't finished with her yet.

'When did you last have a visit from your CPN, Kate? Do you remember?' he wanted to know.

Now, that was definitely a trick question. Of course she remembered. It was a year ago last June when the bossy old bag of a woman had come round with the Home Treatment team. Just before Kate had lost it. Just before her last mini-break at the Belmont. Hadn't seen her since. Hadn't chuffing wanted to. It was always the start of it, the visits from the Community Psychiatric Nurse. Supposed to be the bloody opposite, of course. Supposed to be helpful. How having that bitter control freak who called herself a nurse settling her flabby backside on her mam's sofa once a week was supposed to be helpful baffled Kate. And then it would be twice a week. And then some just-out-of-college daft beggar from the Home Treatment team would start pitching up every couple of days to watch her take her medication. Like she was a chuffing child. Oh aye, she remembered the last time she'd seen her CPN. But it was not a time she wanted to revisit. Didn't want to be talking about that now, not now, not here, not with Doctor Can't-pull-the-wool-over-my-eyes Gregory. But if she said she couldn't remember, what did that say about her state of mind? She decided to hedge her bets.

'Ooh, there's another person'll be rushed off her feet, shouldn't wonder,' she said. 'Don't know how she fits everyone in. Don't you worry about me, Doctor. I'll pop in for the old blood test next week and put your mind at rest.'

He took off his glasses and rubbed his eyes. He looked up at Kate, his head ever so slightly on one side, his pale skin showing early signs of an acne breakout. He did not waste energy on a smile this time.

'It's your mind we want to be at rest Kate,' he told her. 'That's what I'm here for.'

It was on her way out of the surgery, in a state of some grumpiness, that Kate met Teach. He looked, she decided, transparent; he was so thin and pale. She spun him on his bony heel and took him to Luigi's for a bit of fattening up. By the time he had finished his second cheese and ham crostini, Kate had heard to whole sorry tale of the night before. She left the cafe, blood boiling, and went straight to Rufus's flat.

She hammered on the door until her knuckles stung. When he at last appeared the sight of him so obviously hung over and half awake even though it was by now lunch time maddened her further.

'What the chuffing hell do you think you're playing at?' she demanded.

'Since when do I have to explain my actions to you?'

'Since you turned into a feckless bastard, that's when.'

Rufus turned and walked back into the flat. 'If you're going to be abusive,' he said over his shoulder, 'let's not share it with the rest of the block.'

Kate did not move but raised her voice. 'I've seen Teach. I know what you did. How could you? How the chuffing hell could you just stand there and watch when he needed you?'

'He wasn't in any real danger.'

'Oh, that's all right then, isn't it? Doesn't matter he was being bullied, humiliated, threatened, pushed around and generally bloody terrified. Wasn't in any *real danger!*'

Rufus returned to the doorstep in an effort to get Kate to lower her voice. 'Look,' he said, 'you're blowing this thing up out of all proportion. I was with someone.'

'So I hear. Teach said she looked about fifteen.'

'She's twenty-six.'

'Like I give a chuff.'

'Maybe you do. That's what this is really about, isn't it? You're jealous.'

'What?'

'You can't stand the thought of me being happy with someone else.'

'My God, the ego has landed! We finished years ago, and it took me all of five bloody minutes to get over it. Jealous my arse. I pity the poor cow. She has no idea what she's letting herself in for. Bet you haven't told her your little secret, hmmm? Told her about your season ticket to Belmont, have you? About your suicide attempts? Pillow talk like that must be pretty bloody effective, judging by the smug look on your face.'

'Do yourself a favour, Kate, and shut up.'

Kate was shouting properly now. 'Think I'll go and see your little girlfriend. Tell her to keep you away from sharp objects, just to be on the safe side. I'm sure she'd be really turned on by the thought of you...'

Rufus did not let her finish. He grabbed her by the arm and hauled her inside, slamming the door.

'You stay out of it, Kate, you hear? This is none of your business.'

'Do you know how bloody sad you look? Running around pretending to be something... *someone* you're not. Why don't you grow up, Rufus?'

'And why don't you calm down, Kate? You're sounding manic.'

It was all Kate could do not to hit him. 'Don't you dare do that! Don't you dare make out just because I'm angry I'm losing it! I have a right to be chuffing angry, you bastard!'

'And I have a right to live my life how I want.'

'You're a fake, Rufus Waters. You should hate yourself for leaving Teach in the shite like that.'

Rufus rounded on her, teeth gritted. 'You try sex off medication and see how quickly you lose interest in your needy bloody friends. Orgasms, Kate? Remember those, do you? Or has it been too long? Dried up and frigid before your thirtieth birthday. No wonder you're bitchy.'

Kate could feel herself beginning to shake. 'She'll find you out,' she spat the words at him. 'And when she does she'll drop you like the steaming turd you are. You can't just make yourself into someone different. You're stuck with being Rufus the sodding morose bastard, and there's nothing you can do to change it!'

'I can do any damn thing I want. You just watch me!'

CHAPTER TWELVE

Rufus clung to the small, wiry tree that protruded from the cliff, his eyes shut tight.

'It's no good,' he said. 'I can't do it.'

The rope from which he was suspended was taut and, in his opinion, worryingly thin. He forced himself to open his eyes. He looked up, knowing that to look down would be a big mistake. Abigail was at the top of the cliff, peering anxiously over the edge at him.

'You'll be fine,' she said. 'Just relax.'

'Relax!'

'Let go of the tree and push yourself away from the cliff face.'

'I can't.'

'You won't fall, Rufus. Just let yourself slide down.'

'Oh, fuck.'

More climbers appeared at the top, gazing down with pitying expressions. None of them seemed to find the dizzying height a problem. But then none of them was, at that moment, dangling on a piece of string with nothing but a weedy, worm-eaten shrub between them and certain death. Despite the cool wind that was gently buffeting him, Rufus felt horridly hot in his climbing gear. And he looked ridiculous in his crash hat, he knew it. Made his cheeks look hamstery. Motorbike helmets had the same effect. Well, sod it, he wasn't prepared to die looking like a small rodent. Terrified, wimpish, pathetic, a complete sodding coward, maybe. But not hamstery. He offered up a silent prayer to any sympathetic gods that might be having a slow Saturday morning and let go the tree. He snatched at the rope as he whizzed towards the ground. He would have screamed, but did not have time. He landed in an ungainly heap at the bottom of the cliff, amazingly unscathed, save for his battered pride and sweat drenched clothes.

A fellow abseiler stepped forwards to help detach him from the equipment. Abigail's cheery voice sang out above. 'Well done, Rufus! I knew you could do it.'

The fellow abseiler nodded brightly, 'Gets easier the more you do it,' he said. 'You'll be fine next time.'

'I'll take your word for it,' said Rufus, who knew with unshakeable certainty that there would never, under any circumstance, be a next time.

Half an hour later Rufus was sitting glumly in the back of the minibus. Most of the seats were taken up with climbing gear and canoe paddles and numerous other items of torture; the rest were inhabited by the merry little party of which he found himself a member. When Abigail had told him she was going away for a few days' holiday in Wales, and that there was a spare place if he wanted to join them, he had dithered ungallantly. He already knew enough about Abigail to be sure this was not going to be an exploration of Celtic heritage spots, or a leisurely potter around pretty market towns, or a gastronomic tour, perhaps. No, with Abigail it would have to be something most certainly active, probably exhausting, and possibly downright dangerous. He had not, he realised now, anticipated pursuits inducing bollock-shrivelling terror. So short-sighted of him. But then he had been tempted by the thought of a whole mini-break full of nights, and therefore sex, with his new woman. Added to which, he was less than keen on the idea of her sharing so much fresh air and fun with a whole bunch of muscley blokes, however much she insisted they were all just good friends. So he had thought 'what the hell' and said of course he could think of nothing more wonderful. Which was why he was now rattling along a narrow lane somewhere up the arse end of the Brecon Beacons, breathing in sweat, Gortex and testosterone and fervently wishing he had persuaded Abigail that a weekend in a pub in the Cotswolds would have been just as healthy. Not to mention safer. And less group-based. A point that seemed to matter far more to him than it did to her.

Abigail squeezed his hand. 'I'm so glad you decided to come with us. There's loads to do around here. We come every year. You're going to love it.' She paused, then added, 'Don't worry, abseiling's not for everyone.'

Louise, a rosy-cheeked girl with periwinkle eyes and yellow hair piped up. 'Took me ages to get the hang of it. Now you can't keep me off a rock face. And just wait till you try the kayaking!'

'Oh yes,' the shorter of the two men in front of Rufus was called Mike, a Welshman with high energy and a low centre of gravity, 'when you feel that white water all around you, the rocks hurtling by, just you and the river locked in mortal combat... there's nothing like it.'

'I can't wait,' said Rufus.

Abigail smiled at him. 'You did say you'd done a bit before. In Africa,' she pointed out.

'I said I'd been in a canoe. Someone else did the paddling, and there was definitely no white water.'

Mike laughed, 'Still, won't have any hippos to worry about here, will you?'

Abigail all but bounced on her seat. 'Oh Rufus, tell them about the day you saw a crocodile snatch a gazelle from the river bank.'

Rufus caught the unsympathetic exchange of looks between Mike and Dan. Dan frightened Rufus. He was taller than was fair, with lean, hard limbs, and a body that had clearly traded in every inch of fat for muscle some time ago. His dark hair was brutally short, and his stylish goatee gave a saturnine, slightly sinister edge to his appearance. He obviously hadn't packed any casual conversation along with his thermals and wetsuits and had barely spoken two words to Rufus since they had met earlier the same morning. 'Another time, perhaps,' Rufus squeezed Abigail's hand back and smiled, more than a little proprietarily.

The vehicle lurched to a halt. Mike peered through the steamy windows. 'Righto, here we are, then,' he said.

If Rufus had harboured any secret hopes of a gentle flow of sparkling water winding its way down the valley, they disappeared the instant he stepped out of the minibus. The Usk after a week of rain was a brown monster biting chunks out of the riverbanks as it tore past in its great hurry to move quantities of Welsh mud to the nearest bit of sea. It was not, in Rufus's opinion, a place for recreation. It was a place that was very clearly warning off flimsy humans. This was nature doing its dangerous, noisy, cold, terrifying thing, and it was best left to get on with it. The idea that it might be fun to lower oneself into the maelstrom in front of them seemed a purer example of lunacy than anything Rufus had encountered in his long career of madness. He looked desperately at Abigail to remind himself of why he was standing at the water's edge contemplating the impossible. It was humbling to acknowledge that it was lust rather than love that had got him into this predicament. It seemed, suddenly, a very shallow thing to die for. But there was no escape. Canoes were being unloaded by the others with unbridled glee.

Abigail handed him back his crash hat. 'We think it best you share with Dan in one of the two-manners. He's the most experienced canoeist here. He'll look after you,' she assured him.

'Wonderful,' said Rufus. He nodded at Dan, who was far too busy checking the canoe to respond. 'He does take it all very seriously, doesn't he?' he said.

'Oh, he's really competitive, our Dan. Wouldn't surprise me if you two have the best run of all of us.'

'It would amaze me,' muttered Rufus.

The canoes were lowered into the water and after a deal of wobbling Rufus clambered in behind Dan. He felt sick with fear. And more than a little dizzy. And fairly certain he was going to drown, or have his legs smashed against the cruel rocks. Or both, though not necessarily in that order.

Dan turned a smile-free face towards him. 'Just do exactly what I tell you and you might live.'

'I'll hold that thought,' said Rufus glumly, beginning to fear he had stepped into a scene from Deliverance.

With a speed that left him breathless the canoe shot forwards, taken up by the fearsome current, and they were hurtling downstream. Rufus quickly realised that the paddles had nothing to do with propulsion and everything to do with staying alive. Dan barked instructions above the roar of the water, expertly steering the kayak between rocks and through narrow channels. Rufus was too gripped by terror to utter a word. Besides, every time he opened his mouth water found its way in. He clamped it shut, breathing heavily through his nose, struggling to do what Dan told him, fighting the urge to drop his paddle and cling to the sides of the ridiculously flimsy boat. The countryside was a blur. Behind him, during a particularly sharp left-hand bend, he glimpsed the others following in their own canoes. How could anyone actually enjoy this? Why would they voluntarily put themselves through such a lunatic exercise? More than once! Never again was a phrase that was quickly becoming Rufus's personal mantra. The canoe bashed into a lump of granite, jarring every tooth in his head, stalling the forward movement for a fraction of a moment before they plummeted onwards. His arms were aching badly now, and he doubted he could keep up even the pretence of any effectual oarsmanship for much longer. He heard a shout from Dan that had something of an edge and an urgency to it. He looked up to see what had caused The Ice Man to show a glimmer of emotion. He wished he hadn't. There had plainly been some dreadful mistake. Whoever had been responsible for selecting this stretch of river could not have known about the deadly waterfall towards which they were now being carried, flimsy as a leaf, and with about as much chance of survival. Rufus opened his mouth to scream but his voice had already abandoned ship. In a second they were airborne. For an eternal moment of silence the canoe left the water and cut through the air like a missile. Rufus clung to his paddle, and screwed shut every orifice that was still under his control. They rejoined the water like a stone skimmed by a giant, bouncing some considerable distance before slicing into the river again. Dan whooped. Rufus risked opening his eyes. He almost wet himself with relief at the sight of the calm pool into which they had now glided. He was alive! Now that he saw it from his downstream perspective he could see that the waterfall was in fact only a drop of six feet or so. The others were now navigating it with reasonable safety. Nevertheless, he felt a surge of elation and belated adrenaline as he took stock of what he had just managed to do. He raised his paddle above his head, waving it in the air with triumphant shouts of celebration. In doing so he was, unwittingly, destabilising the kayak.

Dan yelled at him, 'Keep still, you moron!'

But it was too late. The canoe teetered, wobbled, and then rolled over. Rufus found himself submerged, upside down, his mouth and nose full of water, his lungs perilously short of air, his oar still clutched in his hand. He tried to wriggle from his seat, but the waterproof apron covering the hole hampered his progress. He was dimly aware of hitting the bottom of the river, and of the canoe landing on top of him, but the water was so churned up and dense with grit that it was impossible to make sense of much. How, he wondered, as he resigned himself to a soggy death, could everything happen in an instant and yet in slow motion at one and the same time? He was just giving in to a curiously welcome sense of giving up, and wondering if Abigail would mourn his passing, when he felt rough hands grabbing him beneath the arms and hauling him upwards. He broke the surface and gulped in air. And more water. As Dan dragged him to the shore he could hear raised voices, one of them Abigail's, calling his name and urging speed. He was manhandled onto the river bank where he lay choking and spluttering, unable to speak, acutely conscious of what a pathetic figure he must cut, and how irritatingly heroic Dan must be looking right about now.

'Rufus!' Abigail's anxious face appeared above him. 'Rufus, you poor thing. Are you all right?'

He fought to reply, to summon some vestige of strength and dignity, to form at least one or two witty words to salvage the situation, and hopefully to prevent Abigail thinking him a complete and utter loser. Instead, all he could do was smile weakly, cough some more, and then roll to one side and vomit loudly on the grass.

The cottage in which the group was staying was very pretty, very small, and very basic. Rufus had hoped for a few creature comforts, a deep, hot bath at the very least, the odd fluffy towel, and perhaps a reviving spot of dinner at a local gastro pub. But, there was to be none of that. Abigail had obviously eschewed comfort and, indeed, the twenty-first century, for cutesville. The little stone building had three draughty bedrooms, a Formica-enhanced kitchen, and a sitting room with a ceiling so low that humans were forced to adopt an unnatural stoop or list to avoid cracking heads on beams. To make the experience complete there was no electricity, and no central heating. Pools of hissing yellow light were provided by gas lamps, and the only heat came from the log fire which belched smoke every time the wind changed direction. Which it seemed to do at ten-minute intervals. Mike and Louise were sitting on one of the small chintz sofas. Rufus and Abigail occupied another. Dan sat stoically on the unyielding wooden chair. Comfort was not something he would have any truck with, Rufus could see that. He fully expected the wretched man to start whittling at any moment. His Iron Man act was really beginning to fray Rufus's nerves, and having had to be rescued by him hadn't helped. He was sure the insufferably smug creature had enjoyed the whole episode. Rufus attempted to slide his arm around Abigail, unable to stop himself wincing as he did so.

'Oh,' Abigail noticed his distress, 'you've really hurt yourself, haven't you?'

'It's nothing, really, just my shoulder.'

Louise spoke up. 'You ought to let Mike take a look at that. He's very good with his hands.'

Mike laughed, 'Don't tell everyone!'

Abigail nodded, 'Louise is right.'

'Come along,' Louise busied herself pulling the coffee table out a little, 'sit yourself down on this.'

'No, thank you,' Rufus shook his head, 'I'd really rather not.'

Louise took his hand and gently but firmly pulled him off the sofa. 'Don't be such a baby. Mike won't hurt you.'

'No more than is absolutely necessary,' Mike grinned, stretching his fingers and making them crack loudly. 'You have my word.' He placed his hands on Rufus's shoulders. He began working the knotted muscles, lightly at first, and then with more force, probing with his thumbs.

'Argh!' Rufus squawked.

'Bingo!' said Mike. 'That's where the problem is. Wrenched a muscle there, you have. Take this thing off and I'll sort it out for you.'

Rufus clutched at his t-shirt. 'Must I?'

'Don't be shy now,' Mike said.

'It's a bit cold in here, that's all.'

'Can't work properly through clothing, you see. Have to feel naked flesh beneath my fingers!' he added with a filthy laugh.

Abigail gave Rufus an encouraging smile. 'Come on,' she said. 'He really is very good. You'll feel heaps better.'

She stood up and reached out to him. Before he could utter a word of protest she had whipped his shirt off over his head. There followed a silence filled with unspoken questions. Even in the blurring gaslight the scars on his upper arms were obvious to everyone. Rufus was unable to move and could think of nothing clever or diverting to say. He avoided meeting Abigail's quizzical gaze.

Mike resumed the treatment. 'Soon have you fighting fit again.'

'Again?' Dan snorted.

Mike ignored him. 'Got to get you in shape for tomorrow morning.'

Rufus focused on the dancing flames of the fire as he spoke. He was relieved that Abigail had gone back to the sofa without commenting on the scars. 'What torture awaits us tomorrow?' he asked.

'Gorge walking!' Mike told him with relish.

'Oh joy.'

Out of the corner of his eye Rufus could see Dan frowning at his arms.

'Looks like you make a bit of a habit of getting yourself damaged,' he said slowly.

Rufus continued to stare into the fire. 'Africa can be a dangerous place,' he said.

'Rufus caught malaria out there,' Abigail explained. 'He still suffers from it sometimes, even now. Sweats and shakes, that sort of thing.'

'Really?' Dan stretched out his long legs. 'Sounds like a junkie I knew once.'

Rufus looked up and glared at Dan. His dislike of the man was quickly intensifying into serious loathing. He put on a bright grin. 'I'm more of your common or garden alcoholic myself,' he said. 'Any more of that beer going, Abigail?'

The tension dissipated, the moment passed. Abigail fetched more bottles of beer, leaning in for a fond kiss as she handed one to Rufus.

CHAPTER THIRTEEN

Quickshopper was unusually busy for a Sunday. Kate had been asked to do an extra shift and had said yes. Why not? Rehearsals were going well; she was pleased with the way her solo was coming along. She was excited about the performance now. A good thing. To be happy. To be looking forward to something. Only problem was, she wasn't sleeping well. Couldn't seem to stay in bed past six o'clock, no matter how late she stayed up, or how much chuffing awful tele she watched into the small hours.

Might as well be busy. Might as well be earning some money. She wanted to have her hair done before the concert, and Snip Snap Snorem didn't work their magic for nothing. Sill, it would be worth it. Brown was boring. Nobody wanted to be brown. Songbirds weren't brown. Songbirds were exotic and colourful and gorgeous. And so she was going to be exotic and colourful and gorgeous. The odd extra shift was just what she needed. Chuffing time and a half too, couldn't whinge about that.

Kate felt good today. There was a spring in her step, despite the rain. What people needed, she decided was more colour in their lives. More fun. 'Wake up and cheer up!' she had shouted at the drawn curtains of the other houses on the estate as she hurried by. She shook rainwater from her hair as she entered the store and set straight to work. She had had a brainwave, a flash of inspiration, one of those why-didn't-I-think-of-that-before moments in the shower, and knew exactly what she needed to do. She was supposed to be on Pet Foods and Barbecue, but that could wait. She was a girl with a mission.

'Hiya!' she waved cheerily at the two girls on the deli counter as she trotted past, her broad smile made all the more striking by the scarlet lipstick she was wearing. 'Another lovely Sunday in Quickshoppers, then! How lucky are we to be working here?' She barely noticed their lack of response, she was too busy greeting customers and pressing packets of chilli spice mix on them. 'Here you are, ladies. Free samples today. Give us five minutes, then pop round to World Food and see what I've got for you. You'll love it, I promise.' She breezed on. The girls on deli exchanged knowing looks and moved further along the counter to get a better view of what Kate was up to

Ten minutes later, when the manager appeared, they were so busy watching her it took them a moment to register his presence. They quickly returned to their duties, eyes cast down. He turned to see what it was that had so taken up their attention. Kate was still animatedly giving away free gifts to somewhat startled shoppers. She wasn't exactly shouting, but her voice had a volume and a force to it that made it carry the length of the aisle.

Mr Morgan moved in for a closer look. When he reached the display Kate had created all he could do was stare, aghast, at the chaotic muddle on the shelves in front of him. Kate was delighted to see him. Now that he was standing next to her he could also see that he was holding an armful of pots of soured cream.

'Mr Morgan! I see you've found my handiwork. What d'you think? You're impressed, I can tell. I'm pretty chuffed with it myself. I was filling up the shelves yesterday – we were dangerously low on Tacos and completely out of the big jars of Salsa. We had small ones, but, between you and me, they're shite really, aren't they? I mean, two blobs on your Tortilla and that's it. Anyway, I spent chuffing ages restocking the shelves, and then this morning, when I was having a shower, 'cause I'm a shower person, me, can't be doing with wallowing about in a bath. Well, you're lying in all your own sweat and muck, aren't you? And who wants to do that? Well, I know some people do, but they want to think about it, really, don't they? Are you a bath person or a shower person? Shower, I reckon, you don't get to be manager by floating about in bits of your own poo, do you? Any road, I was in the shower when I had a revelation. I could see it all, clear as you like, chuffing hell, just the way it should always be. So bloody obvious. I thought, "Duh! Our Katie! Where's your bloody brain been?" So, I got myself down here quick as you like and, not half an hour later, Bob's your mother's brother! I mean, think about it! Use your management salaried bonce and think about it. What's the point of rows of stuff, all separated out? I mean, who wants to be faced with chuffing endless jars of the same thing? I'm not going to eat a whole meal of chilli sauce now, am I? Course not. You want a bit of everything, all together. It makes perfect bloody sense. Look.' She waved one arm expansively at the shelves, still clutching the cream. 'Everything's sorted in little meals, see? There's a selection for your average shopper – one packet of garlic Tortillas, medium spices, kidney beans, large salsa. This one's for the wimps – everything mild, no garlic, no chillies. Sort of Tex Mex without the sex! Ha ha! Oh, and here's one for the serious lover of Mexican food – red hot sauce 'n' spices, two types of beans, spicy salsa. The whole Enchilada. Or almost! One crucial ingredient missing. Did you spot it? No? Not to worry, that's what you've got me for. Look, here you go,' she brandished one of the little tubs in front of him. 'Soured cream! It's so obvious. Let's face it, none of this shite is edible unless you smother it in this stuff, is it?' She began to plonk the pots of cream on the shelves amongst the rest of the food. 'Now, don't start whinging on about the cream not being in the refrigerated unit. This lot'll fly off the shelves faster than you can say stuff my Frajita. There!' She stood back to admire the effect.

Mr Morgan looked at her sadly and sighed the sigh of a man who had been here before.

CHAPTER FOURTEEN

Rufus's long weekend continued on its lurching downward spiral. On his first night in the cottage with Abigail he had been so exhausted and so bruised from his activities, not to mention dangerously jittery due to his abstinence from medication, that sex was out of the question. She seemed unbothered, a fact which only made him feel *more* bothered. He decided his best hope was to redouble his efforts. Whatever torture lay ahead he would face it, manfully, squarely, without a whimper. No matter what.

He had done so pretty darn successfully the next morning, he felt. Gorge walking turned out to be wet, hard on the shins, and pointless, but at least it wasn't terrifying, and he had just about managed to keep up with the others. More than once he had had to resort to delaying tactics – *Was that a kingfisher? Good Lord, Welsh gold! Oh, Abigail, you look tired, sweet thing, stop and have a nibble of my Kendal Mint Cake, why don't you?* – but nobody tutted or rolled their eyes at him, and Deathly Dull Dan was so far ahead he hadn't noticed. The pony trekking had been another matter altogether. Trudging up a rock-infested stream, hour upon hour, was doable, so long as you didn't succumb to boredom. All you had to do was walk, after all. Staying aboard an evil, ginger, Welsh cob whose sole intention was to dump you on the hardest patch of ground it could find was not so simple. For a start, balance was required, something Rufus was lacking, due to the persistent dizziness of his head and blurring of his vision. The other prerequisites for being a successful rider of such hateful beasts appeared to be carbon fibre nerves, a taste for reckless speed on dangerous slopes, and a disregard for the comfort, or even the continued existence, of both bollocks. Rufus knew it was hopeless. It took less than twenty minutes for the horse from hell to rattle him to saddle sore agony before dipping its shoulder, swerving at a non-existent hazard, and depositing Rufus in a nettle-strewn ditch. As a parting gesture it kicked up its iron-clad heels, one of which connected with the little finger of Rufus's right hand, smashing the nail and inflicting a pain so intense he was, at least for a moment, able to forget about the state of his manhood.

By the time he fell into bed on the Sunday night he doubted there were two consecutive square inches of his body that did not hurt. Abigail slid beneath the duvet beside him, still unnervingly fresh and unscathed. She looked at him with undisguised pity.

'I'm sorry,' he said.

'Sorry? What for?'

He waved his bandaged hand in a gesture of hopelessness, 'For being so... well, pants at everything.'

'But it's all new to you. Nobody expects you to be an expert.'

'Thank God.'

'You're just not used to this sort of thing. And your poor hand...' She gently took the swaddled fingers and put them to her lips.

Rufus forced himself not to wince or pull his hand away. 'It's sweet of you to be so understanding,' he said, then added with a sigh, 'I really wanted this holiday to be special, for both of us.'

'And it is. We're here, together, getting to know each other.' She grinned, 'Anyway, you'll love tomorrow, couldn't fail to.'

'What can be left? Naked paragliding, perhaps?'

She laughed. 'What a fantastic idea!'

'I think you like torturing me.'

'Relax. We're going for a walk, silly.'

'Really? Just a walk? Nothing life-threatening involved? No rope bridges? Quicksand? Wolves?'

'Just a walk up a mountain. What could be hard about that?' She snuggled closer.

Rufus stroked her hair and bit his bottom lip thoughtfully. She was so pretty, so kind, so sympathetic. He thought for a moment longer then drew a steadying breath. 'You know, Abi, I really like you. You are a sweet girl. The thing is, I think it's only fair to tell you, I've had a change in my medication lately.'

'For the malaria?'

'Not exactly, no. There's something else. Something you don't know about.'

Abigail stayed close. 'Oh? What is it? You know you can tell me.'

'I want to, it's just that, well, sometimes people don't understand. They sort of jump to conclusions.' When she didn't respond he went on. 'The thing is, my father died when I was a teenager, and I didn't cope at all well. In fact, it screwed me up. I started having panic attacks. Depressive phases. Suicidal urges. The whole bang shoot. I was dragged off to a shrink. Then given happy pills, you know the sort of thing. I was very young. Anyway, I'd get better for a while, then worse again. Good times and bad times. And that's how it's been ever since, to tell the truth. On a good day I'm your regular guy. On a bad day I'm... not. So, I've been in and out of the Belmont a bit.'

'The mental hospital?'

'Yes.'

'I see,' she said. 'Why didn't you tell me any of this before?' A thought hit her. 'Was it all lies? The malaria? Africa? The book?'

'No! Well, yes, some of it. Look, I'm sorry. I didn't want to lie to you, it's just.... put it this way, I've had people respond badly to the truth in the past.'

'And you thought I would too?'

'I needed to get to know you first, before I tried to explain.'

A difficult silence joined them in the bed. Abigail pulled away a little and turned her face to him. He saw a mixture of hurt and concern and hated himself even more than usual.

'Are you still having treatment?' she asked.

'No, actually. I'm coping on my own now. Haven't been near the Bin for ages. Doing quite well, I think. I hope. But it isn't easy.'

'Tell me,' she said. 'Tell me what it's like.'

Rufus shook his head. It was impossible. How could he ever explain? Where would he start? But then, he so wanted her to understand. Her took her hand in his good one and stroked her palm with his thumb as he spoke. 'When I'm OK, when I'm *normal*... not depressed, I suppose I mean, even then, if you're a depressive, it's with you. Like the lingering smell of cigarette smoke on your clothes. It never completely goes away. You're always conscious of the fact that it could take over your life again, at any moment. It's a bit like having a stalker; you're forever looking over your shoulder. You look for the signs, the little shifts in your own way of being in the world. And they are so sodding subtle. You know, there is a moment, just before you drop into the stinking black slime of depression proper, a moment when you feel completely, utterly weightless. As if gravity has ceased to exist. Like the fraction of a second when you step off a cliff or a window ledge, I should imagine. Before you plummet. It is a glimpse of bliss, really it is. A tiny peek at what it must be like to be free of the dragging weight of your body and the even heavier sodding weight of your mind. Your fickle, faithless mind. The mind that waits until you are looking the other way and then shoves you towards that plunge, that descent. That's when I feel most mad, actually. Not when I'm in a depression. I can't articulate the thought "I am a loon" then. But in that frozen moment there is a terrifying self-awareness. You *know*, with diamond clarity you can *see*, that you are set apart from everybody else. That you are not of this world. That nothing is really as it seems. That it is all a dream, a nightmare, a joke. And that you are losing your mind because now you can see this. And you will never make anyone else see it. Nobody else will ever understand. It is the loneliest feeling on earth. You feel dizzy, dazzled by this obvious, inescapable truth. Somehow you have been delivered to the wrong planet, the wrong species, the wrong place in time and space, and you will never find your way home. And then you fall.' Rufus could say no more. He felt ridiculous tears stinging his eyelids. He sniffed them away, fairly convinced Abigail would already have him down as a self-pitying freak, but not wanting to confirm this assessment of his character.

To his surprise she squeezed his hand and gave him a small, hopeful little smile. 'I'm glad you told me,' she said, before nestling back into him.

Rufus felt tension and angst draining from his body. He hugged her close. 'So am I,' he said. 'So am I.'

The next morning the rain had stopped and only small clouds dithered about overhead trying to decide whether to rain or drift away. Rufus took a stroll around the garden, mug of coffee in hand, allowing himself to feel just a smidge pleased with how Abigail had taken his revelation of the night before. There was hope after all, it seemed. He was heading back inside the cottage when he heard Abigail's voice from the other side of a piece of trellis. He squinted through the honeysuckle and spotted her and Dan putting out the rubbish bags. He opened his mouth to speak but, still unaware of his presence, Dan beat him to it.

'So, how is Action Man this morning?' he asked Abigail.

'Do you have to be so hard on him? He's doing his best.'

'I don't like him, Abi. And I don't trust him.' Dan jammed the lid on the rubber bin. 'There's something fake about him.'

'No, you're wrong,' she said. 'It's just that...'

'Go on.'

'He's not well.'

'You don't believe all that malaria crap do you?'

'We talked last night. He's had some problems. Mental health problems.'

'I knew it!' Dan snorted, 'Fucking Looney Toons.'

'He suffers from depression, that's all.'

'That's all!'

'He's really on top of his condition now. Hasn't needed to go into hospital for ages.'

Rufus didn't know whether the way his heart was constricting was because of Abigail so sweetly sticking up for him, or because he knew she hadn't a cat in hell's chance of convincing anyone.

Dan was predictably unmoved. 'Listen, Abi, the minute you get home dump this loser. I'm telling you now, there's no future in nurse-maiding some fruitcake.'

'He's really a lovely person. I do like him,' she said in a voice that was becoming smaller and fainter with every word.

'You can't have a proper relationship with someone like that. Have you thought about this? Seriously? What would you do if he tried to top himself? Or turned violent? You don't know what's going on in that screwed up head of his.'

'Oh, I'm sure he's not dangerous.'

'Maybe he is, maybe he isn't. Point is, you will never be sure. You've got to ditch him. You know I'm right, don't you?'

'I don't know,' Abigail was barely audible now, and Rufus had to lean into the climbing shrubs to catch her words. 'It seems such a shame...'

'Abi!' Dan insisted. 'Don't get yourself mixed up with someone like that. You'll get hurt. He's not worth it. You'll have to dump him. OK?'

'I suppose you're right,' she said with a sigh.

Rufus stood motionless until the others had returned inside and closed the kitchen door behind them. He felt utterly betrayed. How could she so easily give up on him? He knew how. He knew he shouldn't be surprised. A familiar heaviness settled about his shoulders. For a few short hours he had allowed himself to believe that this time, *this time*, with this girl, he could be honest. It would be OK. But no. No.

An hour later he found himself disembarking from the minibus at the bottom of a vertiginous grassy incline. It started to rain heavily.

'Here we are!' Abigail waved her arms at the murky mountain. 'Bron-y-Big. I love this walk. Lovely gentle slopes, whinberries, cotton grass, heather, and views to die for.'

Rufus gazed about him at the descending cloud and said nothing. All the fight had gone out of him. He felt sick. His head ached abominably. His vision was blurry and his skin itchy. A deadening lethargy had taken over his limbs. Every scratch, bump, and bruise hurt. His bandaged hand appeared to be three times its normal weight. At that moment, no amount of bright-eyed enthusiasm or sunny smiles from Abigail could lift his spirits. He knew she didn't mean any of it. She was just like the rest of them. She couldn't cope with him. Couldn't handle the truth. Couldn't be arsed. Well, stuff her. All he wanted to do was get home, and if he had to slog up a sodden sodding Welsh mountain first then so be it. The image of his cosy, peaceful, warm and dry flat flashed before his eyes.

'Right!' he said. 'Let's get on with it.'

The others looked on in bewilderment as he strode off, head down.

Within minutes they had all overtaken him. The higher the path took him, the more halting his progress became. The thin air seemed to be fifty percent water, as they ascended into the dense cloud snagged by the stony peak of Bron-y-Big. Soon Dan and Mike were out of sight. Abigail and Louise slowed their pace to stay with Rufus, a fact that made him feel even more pathetic. When Abigail nipped behind a rock for a pee he slumped to the ground, labouring to drag air in and out of his burning lungs.

Louise looked down at him thoughtfully. 'I know what they are,' she said. 'Those scars on your arms. I know what they are.'

Rufus was too surprised by the remark to form a reply.

'Don't worry,' she went on, 'Abigail doesn't. She'd never understand something like that.' She turned to walk on, then paused, adding, 'Mine are on my legs.'

Rufus watched her disappear into the mist. Abigail's sudden reappearance at his side made him jump. He stood up shakily.

'Are you all right?' she asked.

'Perfectly fine, thank you.'

'You're very quiet this morning. Is anything wrong?'

'What could possibly be wrong? Come on, we're getting left behind.'

The weather quickly worsened. Rufus leaned into the rain and the wind as the weather tried its best to force him back down the hill. Down the slippery slope of life. Well, fuck it. He would get to the top. He would tell them all they were a boring bunch of bigots, and he would go home.

'Rufus?' Abigail touched his elbow. 'Are you sure you're OK? You're breathing very heavily.'

'I'm... walking up... a... bastard.... mountain.'

'We could stop. Have a rest.'

'No… thank you.'

'Look, you don't have to do this. We could go back down if you like. Wait for the others in the minibus.'

'No way!' he paused to speak, unable to walk and express how pissed off he was at the same time. 'I'm not going to give

Dung-brained Dan the fucking satisfaction! I'm going to beat this sodding mountain if it kills me!' He pressed on, Abigail following a few steps behind. Their destination was entirely obliterated by cloud. Indeed, visibility in any direction was reduced to a few metres. So much for the fabulous fucking views! After a further hour of struggle Rufus glimpsed a flash of red gortex up ahead. Now he could see the others sitting by the cairn, drinking their disgusting energy drinks. 'Yes! I'm not going to let some slimy lump of rock and sheep shit beat me!'

Abigail caught him up to congratulate him. 'Well done, Rufus! I knew you could do it. Rufus?'

'It's all right,' he wheezed at her, 'you can drop the pretence now. You thought I'd fail, just like everybody else did. Because I'm a useless nutter, aren't I? And nutters are a dead weight. Not worth bothering with. Well, fuck a lot of that!' he cried, before keeling over, face ashen, a combination of hyperventilation, exhaustion, lack of sleep, and absence of medication finally overcoming him. He fumbled in his pocket and whipped out a paper bag. He raised it to his mouth, but the wet wind snatched it from his hand. He watched it, wide-eyed, as it took flight and disappeared. The dark grey of the Welsh day darkened into blackness as he lost consciousness.

When he came to he was alarmed to find himself wrapped in an exposure blanket and cradled in Dan's lap. He wriggled feebly, the metallic fabric rustling and making him feel like an oven-ready chicken. Just as ridiculous and just as hopeless. Stuffed, in fact.

'Don't try to get up.' He could hear Abigail above the whine of the wind. 'Help is on its way.'

Help, when it arrived, turned out to be of the startlingly

dramatic kind. A cacophonous red helicopter emerged through the gloom and settled on the peaty ground. Rufus squinted woozily as two members of Thunderbirds International Rescue leapt from the aircraft and ran towards him. He half wondered why nobody said 'F.A.B'. By the time he had been heaved onto a stretcher and had an oxygen mask strapped to his face his humiliation was complete. As he was lifted into the helicopter he caught a glimpse of Abigail's face. He closed his eyes against the confusion and pity he saw there, and passed out once more.

CHAPTER FIFTEEN

Rufus slammed the front door of his flat behind him and made straight for the kitchen shelf where he kept his booze. His right hand trailed its grubby bandage. He took down a bottle of Remy Martin and unscrewed the top. The light on the answerphone blinked reproachfully at him as he swigged from the bottle. He pressed the play button and leant against the wall, still swigging.

Kate's voice had an edge to it. 'Well? Are you still alive, Mr Outward-Chuffing-Bound? If you are, ring me, OK? If you're not, lucky us. Lucky you. Bastard.'

The second message was from Matthew.

'Hello there, baby brother. Just checking in. We haven't seen you for a while. Helen's been baking. I need help with a truly gargantuan fruitcake. Well, give us a call when you have a mo'. Bye, then.'

His mother was less cheery. 'Rufus? Please don't pretend you're not there, it's too tiresome. Rufus! Really!'

Rufus switched off the machine and trudged over to the CD player. Even amid his preferred untidiness, he was able to put his hand straight on the piece of music he sought. He turned up the volume and, without bothering to remove his coat, planted himself in his leather dentist's chair, reclining at an angle which allowed both collapse and drinking. He closed his eyes and let Albinoni's *Adagio* float over him. A gentle wave of singing strings, the minor key and exquisite balance of tempo and pitch produced the most melancholy sound on earth. And he loved it. It entered his whole being and connected exactly with the vibrations of his own psyche. There was nothing else, no other piece of music, no other utterance or song made by man or nature that could so completely and precisely connect with him. Especially now. Especially at these times. When he felt like this. When the leaden monster had taken up residence in his belly once again. The pressure inside his brain threatened to explode his skull. It was as if his whole subconscious self was suddenly, terrifyingly awake. Awake and screaming. Screaming at him to run, or to fight, or to kill, or to fuck, or something. Something! It was too soon, surely? Too soon to have fallen this far. He had expected a longer battle with his head, more time to fight. But now he seemed to be lurching into the abyss. No! He wouldn't let it happen. He wouldn't be sucked down into that treacly blackness. Abruptly he sat up, spilling brandy as he clambered off the chair. He hurried to the coffee table and knelt on the polished floorboards. He slid his hand beneath the table top and released a tiny catch. A slim drawer, concealed in the framework of the piece of furniture, slid open with a soft click. He pulled it out to its full extent. A shiver of excitement, of anticipation, ran the length of his spine. He touched the collection of knives and blades in front of him, letting his fingers trace their slender metal shapes. Quickly he took off his coat and removed his t-shirt. He drank more brandy, then sat on the floor, his back against the sofa, and picked up a shiny new razor blade. Slowly, with infinite care, he placed the edge of the blade against his upper arm. He applied a little pressure. For an instant there was nothing, then dark blood sprang from the cut. With one gradual, deliberate movement, he drew the blade downwards, slicing into his skin, watching the rivulet of blood forming and then flowing. He was dimly aware of a sharp pain, hot, penetrating, and then the longed for release. A letting go. A silent sigh of relief. The throbbing in his head subsided. The panic pressing on his chest eased. The sensation of building terror was replaced by a weighty sadness. Crucially, a calm, weighty sadness. He cut again. A loving stroke with the blade. Blood dripped onto the floor. He dropped the blade, took another swig of brandy, and closed his eyes, willing unconsciousness to take him. As it did his mind began to freefall, tumbling and spinning, snatching at clouds of thought and memory as it descended. He saw himself in a coffin, being lowered into his own grave. Looking up he could clearly see his family watching him being interred. Matthew wept soundlessly. Lydia checked her watch.

Rufus opened his eyes, fighting against his brain's choice of vision. He steadied himself with deep breaths and then squinted as an apparition came into focus. On the other side of the room, Dr Spinks reclined on enormous, richly embroidered cushions. He wore a maroon silk smoking jacket in paisley print and a scarlet fez. Beside him sat an enormous brass and glass hookah pipe, through which he smoked hashish, languidly inhaling and exhaling pungent smoke. Rufus rubbed his eyes, but Dr Spinks remained where he was.

'Hey, Rufus! Good to see you. It's been a while. I've missed our little chats. Always liked you, Rufus. You were always one of my favourites. You knew that, didn't you?' He paused to savour another lungful of the sweet fumes from the pipe. 'You know, your really don't look good at all. Not at all. And, aw, Rufus, look what you've done to yourself.' He gesticulated with a lazy hand. 'Now, we talked about this, didn't we? Hmm, didn't we? And you promised me. "No more cutting," you said.' Dr Spinks sighed heavily and wriggled into an even more comfortable position, sinking still deeper into his cushions. 'I understand how hard things are for you right now, believe me, I do. But you know you only have to ask and you can have exactly the drugs you need. Why make life harder? I'm here to help, Rufus.'

As he spoke the doctor slowly started to grow fatter. First a little plump, then worryingly bloated, then obese, then obscenely corpulent. His skin wobbled and took on a bilious lime hue. Rufus stared, transfixed, as the man in front of him metamorphosed into a giant green caterpillar, still wearing the fez and smoking the pipe. Rufus attempted to recoil, but his back was against the sofa, and his limbs refused to respond to the desperate, but strangely distant, urgings of his mind. He shut his eyes, turning to bury his head against his arm, the sound of the abominable creature's throaty laughter filling his mind as he mercifully passed out.

Rufus was awoken by the sound of thumping on the door and his name being called. He was surprised to find he had somehow made it into his bed, a bed that was horribly tangled and sweaty. He struggled to surface, not allowing himself to revisit the nightmares of the previous day. Recognising Teach's voice, he stumbled towards the door, scooping up his t-shirt on the way and dragging it over his head. He fought with the locks and found Teach standing outside clutching three overstuffed carriers and coughing elaborately.

'Hail fellow, well... my word, Ruf! You do look dreadful.'

'Good to see you too, Teach.' He shuffled back inside, Teach following him towards the kitchen area. The light on the answerphone flashed accusingly. Rufus pressed the button.

'This is a message for Rufus Waters. I'm calling from the Herald. We were expecting Rufus back at work yesterday, but...'

He did not wait to hear more. He wrenched the machine from the table and flung it at the opposite wall. A brief moment of noise as it smashed and fell was followed by a loaded silence. Rufus set about making tea, his movements deliberate and painfully slow, his shaking making the simplest tasks a challenge.

Teach carefully set down his bags. 'Thought you must be back by now, hadn't seen you for ages, so just, you know, thought I'd drop by.'

Rufus steadied himself against the worktop. 'What day is it?' he asked.

'Wednesday, far as I can tell.'

'What the fuck happened to Monday and Tuesday?'

'Ah, *tempus fidget*. I lost whole weeks back in the seventies. Come to think of it, I pretty much lost the seventies. I've got photographs, though...'

Rufus handed a milkless mug of tea to Teach, took one for himself, and padded over to the sofa. He flopped down, wincing, not sure which of his various afflictions was the most painful. Teach sat cross-legged on the rag rug the other side of the coffee table. Rufus looked at him properly, trying to bring his mind into the room.

'I'm sorry,' he said, 'you know. About what happened.'

Teach fought his way through a bout of coughing, waving a dismissive hand. 'All forgotten. Water under the fridge.' He took his tobacco tin out of his jacket pocket and began to roll a joint.

Rufus sipped some tea and burned his lip. 'It's just, well, I was with this girl,' he felt a powerful need to explain. And to have Teach understand. To have Teach forgive him. 'It was our first date.'

'Oh, yes, very pretty, I thought. How is that going?'

'It's gone. I blew it completely.'

'Oh, surely not.'

'Kate was right. I can't do it. I can't operate out there in the world of real, normal people. I just fuck up.' He found a brandy stain on his t-shirt and rubbed at it, unable to lift his eyes. 'I failed, Teach. It's as simple as that.'

'Think you're being a bit hard on yourself there, Ruf. *Nil desperado.* Could be too soon to tell.' He licked the cigarette papers and his fingers rolled expertly.

'Look, the holiday with Abigail was a disaster. One sodding humiliation after another. And for what? She was no different from all the others. Who was I trying to kid? I can't even hold down a pathetically feeble little job.'

'At least you tried. Nothing ventured...'

'Teach, please.'

'Right, sorry. Absolutely understand.'

They sat in silence. Teach slurped his tea to quell another fit of coughing. Rufus let numbness overwhelm him.

'So,' Teach spoke with the unlit joint between his teeth, 'what will you do now?' He glanced down at the floor between them.

Rufus followed the direction of his gaze. The dried blood had formed small maps of misery on the wooden boards. Instinctively Rufus tugged at the sleeve of his shirt. 'That's the point,' he said, 'I don't *do* anything. And that's the way I'll spend the rest of my pointless existence, I suppose. Not doing. Thinking, yes, feeling, watching, but never actually doing anything, because if I do, that's when it all unravels. I don't live a life at all; I just watch other people living lives, like some endless, dull, badly written movie. So I don't think I'll bother trying any more, thank you very much.'

'Ruf, I may be talking out of turn here, so please, tell me to shut up and mind my own business. Don't want to overstep the mark, wouldn't dream of telling you what to do. Nothing worse that unwanted advice...'

'For fuck's sake, Teach.'

'OK. Yup, come to the point,' he lit the joint, took a deep toke, then spoke through a held breath. 'I should pay your old friend Dr Spinks a visit. See if he has any ideas.'

Rufus parried a caterpillar-shaped flashback.

'Like I say,' Teach went on, 'none of my business.' He leaned forward and offered the joint to Rufus, who merely shook his head. Teach nodded, then resumed smoking. Outside the weather had worsened and soon the only sounds in the room were the window panes being stung by the rain and the low rumble of Teach's chest. At last he said, 'So, it's the big day soon.'

Rufus frowned at him.

'The Belmont Choir Concert,' Teach explained. 'Highlight of the Hereford cultural calendar. Kate's getting excited about it already. In fact, Kate's more than a little excited about everything just now.'

'Really?'

'You know how she can be.'

Rufus would not meet his eye. 'I know she's not above letting us put her bizarre behaviour down to her condition when it suits her,' he said.

'Ah, yes, using her mania as an escape goat. Still, I'm sure she'd be thrilled skinny to see you.'

'Somehow I doubt it,' said Rufus, turning to gaze towards the window and watch the watery mess that the day had already become.

By the time he set off along the riverbank two hours later the rain had properly set in. He had recognised the necessity for a coat, but had somehow not carried this thought through as far as a hood or hat. Consequently his head was now taking the brunt of the downpour, his hair slick against it. He stuffed his hands deep into his pockets and proceeded, head down, in an uneven march. He had no clear plan of where he was going or why he was walking, he knew only that he must. The river was swollen and fast-flowing. All along the bank the lower branches of willows were being sucked down and pulled from the trees. Forlorn water birds paced the grassy shores, not daring to return to the dangerous water. Rufus cared about none of this. He marched on until at length he came to the iron footbridge. A sign had been erected declaring it unsafe. Striped tape criss-crossed the entrance. Rufus pushed past the sign and ducked beneath the tape. He strode across the bridge, a man of unknown purpose. When he came to the halfway point he stopped. He turned to lean over the rail, the flaking paint on the rusting ironwork gritty beneath his palms. He glazed down at the angry water below. Deep, fast, deadly water. His hands tightened on the rail, his grip whitening his knuckles, his jaw set, his breath held. Then, suddenly, the fight went out of him. As if a switch had been thrown. A plug pulled. He felt such a draining of energy, such a lack of power that his legs could barely support him. He staggered back off the bridge as if under a weight so tremendous it might press him to the ground. He might lie there, suffocating beneath it, too spent, too flimsy, too insubstantial to move. The desire to lie down was alarmingly strong. He forced himself to walk on, on drunken legs, back along the footpath, back towards the city centre, back towards what life he had.

In Chipton Street he came across a small French cafe. He went inside and landed heavily on a seat by the window. He sat for a moment, motionless, his breathing shallow, water dripping from his hair onto the table. A bone-numbing coldness took hold of him, and he began to shiver. When a waitress appeared with notebook and pencil he somehow managed to express his need for coffee. The cafe was busy, almost full. People chatted, or read newspapers, or fed themselves, or admonished small children. Nobody took any notice of Rufus. He gazed out through the rain-lashed window. Outside shoppers bustled by. As he watched, their movements became increasingly rapid. Faster and faster they went, back and fore, until they were passing the window in a wet blur, speeded up, their jerky walking and scurrying faster and more ridiculous than a precinct of Keystone Cops, their blank faces unseeing and expressionless as they rushed by. Rufus wanted to scream, to cry out to them, to beg them to stop their madness, to slow down. His own actions, in contrast, were leadenly slow. There appeared to be a different strength of gravity surrounding him, exerting a pull so strong that only with supreme effort was he able to raise a hand and press it against the glass. The shoppers sped on, heedless of his despair, blind to his gesture of helplessness. When he looked back into the room he found his coffee had been placed in front of him. His hands were shaking so badly now he was unable to tear open the sugar wrapper. He picked up his spoon, rattling it against the cup as he struggled to stir the frothy drink so that it might cool quicker.

A middle-aged woman in a red mackintosh approached Rufus's table. Rufus frowned at her. He could see her mouth was open and her lips were moving. He knew she must be speaking. Speaking to him. But he could hear no discernible words. Only fuzzy, indecipherable sounds.

'I'm sorry? What?' he said, his tongue thick in his mouth.

The woman continued to spew gibberish at him. She flapped her hand at the empty seat at his table, smiling and insistent, clearly waiting for a response.

Rufus staggered to his feet, his chair tumbling over backwards; the table jogged, spilling coffee in a steaming flood of its own. Others turned to stare. The woman looked concerned, stepping closer, still talking. Rufus shook his head, backing away, desperate to escape, alarmed and confused, terrified that soon they would notice, in a second they would see that their was an alien being in their midst. A freak. A monster. A creature not of their world. Not in any way like them. He pushed past the startled woman, shoving her aside as he blundered out of the cafe and back into the incessant rain.

CHAPTER SIXTEEN

Dr Spinks's surgery felt, to Rufus, even more inappropriately glamorous and perfect than usual. It was thrown into sharp relief by his own dirty and dishevelled state. He allowed himself to be shepherded through the door by the lovely Marion. The doctor advanced, hand outstretched.

'Hi, Rufus! Good to see you. Come on in. Sit down, sit down. You look tired.'

Rufus shook his hand limply and subsided into the nearest chair. He closed his eyes against a singularly vivid flashback of Dr Spinks as a fez-wearing caterpillar. When he dared open them again he took care to focus on his feet, keeping both his psychiatrist and any threatened hallucinations on the very periphery of his vision. Even so he was aware of the other man's customary pose, elbows on desk, fingertips together, expression open and eager and ready to listen.

'So, Rufus, tell me what you have been doing. How have you been? I've missed our little chats.'

Rufus was unable to stop himself glancing up. To his relief, Dr Spinks remained reasonably human. The silence between them broadened. The doctor waited, and Rufus searched for a way to express himself; to convey his sense of hopelessness and despair; to intimate to this man-who-is-supposed-to-understand that his mind was imploding and his soul in torment, that he wished he were dead but lacked the courage needed to end his miserable life. He wanted to tell him of the weight of sadness that was pressing down upon him so heavily that at moments he could barely stand. He wanted to hurl himself into the older man's arms and sob until he had no tears left. To be comforted. To be soothed. To be loved, as he was, in all his wretchedly imperfect state. He summoned a flimsy voice.

'Things... didn't work out,' he said.

'I'm sorry to hear that, Rufus. Would you like to tell me more?'

Rufus shrugged. 'What else is there to say? I failed. I couldn't hack it.'

Dr Spinks cocked his head sympathetically. 'You mustn't feel defeated just because you need a little help. Everybody needs someone to talk to. And, in certain cases, that someone happens to be a professional such as myself. It's not so strange, really, is it now? And you know, an awful lot of people who don't have long term mental health problems still take medication from time to time.' He stood up and walked to the window, looking out at the sky of battleship grey. The clouds momentarily parted a fraction, as if even they could not resist his charm, and a few sunny rays of hope broke through, back-lighting the good doctor with an evanescent halo. 'I understand your wish to be free of the stigma that is attached to an illness of this nature, Rufus. Believe me, you are not the first of my patients to try sustained denial and positive thinking as a cure. But you know, it really isn't necessary to put yourself through such an ordeal.' He gave a little sigh. 'It's a disappointingly unenlightened world we live in, I know. There are good people out there, but they simply do not understand.' He turned to face Rufus. A rueful smile drifted across his face. 'Pretending isn't the answer, is it? It's all a question of controlling the condition, and not allowing it to control you.' He glided over to where Rufus was sitting, leaned forward, and gave him a reassuring pat on the knee. 'I'm always here for you, Rufus.'

Rufus stared at the hand, unable either to move or respond.

'So,' Dr Spinks moved over to his desk and picked up his prescription pad, 'we'll start you back on your medication, nice and slow, shall we? I'll have Marion fix up another appointment for you to come and see me in a couple of days. How'd that be?' He signed his name with a flourish looked up, beaming.

Rufus felt his whole body sag, as if he had been filleted.

'Fine,' he found himself saying. 'That'll be fine.'

'Good man!' Dr Spinks spoke into his intercom, 'Oh, Marion, could you please bring your appointment book in here? And some of your wonderful coffee would be fantastic right now. What d'you say, Rufus?'

Rufus forced himself to stand up. 'No,' he said. 'No, thank you. There is somewhere I have to be.'

The rain had eased to a drizzle, no doubt saving itself for further storms later on. Rufus turned up his collar, jammed his hands in his pockets, and hurried the short distance to the Cathedral. As he eased open the door he could hear sublime singing already in progress. He made his way to a pew near the back as quietly as he could. The choir were in full voice, reaching the rousing crescendo of the second movement of Handel's *Messiah*. As the audience applauded Rufus squinted through the serried ranks of singers until he found Kate. Her appearance disturbed him. Although she was wearing the same black trousers and burgundy shirt uniform as the rest of the choir there was something in the way she wore it, something in the inappropriately unbuttoned blouse, the rolled back cuffs, the profusion of costume jewellery, the high-gloss scarlet lipstick, the pink scarf that vaguely secured her chaotic hair on top of her head. Hair that seemed to have developed rainbow streaks. This was not steady Kate, calm Kate, peaceful Kate, damn it – *normal* Kate. This was Kate on the brink of flight. Kate about to leave her earthbound self and take to the stratospheric heights of her mania. Kate about to lose it.

The choir director twitched his baton and Kate edged to the front. Her eyes bright, she held her score in front of her, took a breath, and began to sing. And how she sang! The opening bars of Purcell's masterpiece were low and sombre, drawing the listener in, inviting intimacy and closeness. Kate had perfect control of her exquisite voice. Even in her racing, whirling, frenetic state, when she sang she was as in command of her self as it was possible for a person to be. Not a note was hurried. Not a word misshapen. Not a nuance missed. As the melody leapt to its mournful, heartbreaking, dissonant high notes Kate reached every beat effortlessly.

> *When I am laid, am laid in earth,*
> *May my wrongs create no trouble,*
> *No trouble in thy breast.*
> *Remember me. Remember me.'*

The audience was enraptured. Spellbound. Rufus watched all those sane, sensible people watching Kate. He saw them nod their approval, saw them delight in her voice, saw them moved by her talent, saw them love her. And tears rolled unchecked down his face, blurring his vision. Everybody in the cathedral, just for those few moments, took Kate and her magic into their hearts. Kate sang, Dido lamented, imploring all who heard her to remember her, and Rufus knew that his dear friend was every bit as doomed as Purcell's tragic heroine, and he wept for both of them. He wept for all of them.

As the concert came to an end there was sustained, enthusiastic applause. The choir began to disperse and Kate spotted Rufus. She waved excitedly and hurried over to him.

'Hi!' she threw her arms around him and kissed him hard, leaving him breathless and with a bleeding lip. Kate spoke as if in some sort of race, gesticulating all the while. 'Brilliant you could make it. Wasn't sure you'd show up, flaky bugger. Course it would have been better if you'd been singing with us, but well, that's you being you, isn't it? Weren't we fucking fantastic, though? Didn't you think? That has to be the best we've ever sung. Did you hear the applause? Everyone loved it. Every last stuck-up bugger loved it, didn't they? Hey, Brian!' she waved at two fellow choristers, 'Amanda! Fucking well done! We slayed 'em in the aisles. Ha, ha!' She paused to signal thumbs up to other singers. Members of the audience turned to see where all the noise was coming from. The verger hovered anxiously behind a pillar. People began to melt away as Kate's voice continued to echo around the cathedral. Rufus took her arm and steered her towards the door.

'So,' Kate tugged the scarf from her head, letting her unwashed hair fall messily about her shoulders. 'Little Miss Adventure not with you then? Rumbled you already, has she? Or are you on to the next one? You know what they say: a man's as sane as the woman he feels. Right, I'm chuffing starving. All that singing. We were bloody good though, don't tell me you weren't stunned. I can see you were.'

'You were great,' said Rufus.

'Great? We were fucking fantastic!'

They left the cathedral, Kate's words ricocheting off the walls behind them. They walked across the damp, jewel green grass, Kate talking ceaselessly.

'Let's get a takeaway. What d'you fancy? Chinese, let's have Chinese. No, I'm too hungry. Fish and Chips, that's it. Come on, let's be chuffing British.'

The next half hour saw them queueing agitatedly at the chip shop, calling at the off licence, and striding briskly through the shiny wet streets to Rufus's flat. Once inside Rufus fetched glasses and a corkscrew and slumped on the sofa. He let Kate spread the food on the coffee table while he poured the wine. He found his appetite even more feeble than was normal of late. Somehow Kate's energy was draining him. He nibbled at a chip, forcing it down with a good swig of Cote du Rhone, as Kate ate and drank with enormous enthusiasm. Her endless chattering continued, making him wonder how she didn't choke on her fish.

'So, tell all,' Kate wanted to know as she knelt on the rag rug, jigging and fidgeting as she grabbed handfuls of chips. 'Did she dump you, or was it the other way around? Bet she dumped you. Don't take that the wrong way; it's just how things chuffing are. The world is divided into two types as far as bloody hopeless couples go. Believe me, I know, I've been the dump*ee* far more often than the buggering dump*er.* It's our lovely little lot in life, isn't it? Here, don't be tight with the wine, Rufus. Why is it people with money are always stingy? Anyway, you needn't think getting the push is always 'cos you're a certified loonie like me. You can't blame all your pathetic short-chuffing-comings on your mental health problems. I don't.' She washed down more chips with more wine. Rufus had given up any pretence of eating and was sitting motionless, powerless to resist the onslaught of Kate's stream of consciousness.

'Point is,' she went on, 'there's no use whingeing and whining on about suffering from depression, or mania, or paranoia, or whatever, you just have to get on with it. If people don't like it, fuck 'em. Mmm, good fish. Aren't you going to eat yours? Rich bastards are so chuffing wasteful too, have you noticed that? No, don't suppose you have. Should see it where I work. They come into the supermarket and buy trolleys full of stuffed olives and pesto and water biscuits and other pretentious crap. Bet they never eat chuffing half of it. What is the point of a water biscuit, anyway, will someone please tell me that?'

Kate screwed up the empty paper from her fish supper and threw it across the floor. Rufus watched it bounce off the stuffed squirrel. She stood up and walked round the coffee table and, without pausing, sat astride him, removing her blouse over her head in one swift movement. Rufus was too stunned to protest. It was only when she reached behind her back to unfasten her bra that he found his voice.

'Kate! What are you doing?'

'Duh! Taking my clothes off?' With a ping her bra came undone. It whistled past Rufus's ear as she tossed it over the back of the sofa.

'I can see that,' he said, shrinking back against the leather, 'but why?'

Kate shrugged. 'I like to have sex with my clothes off. But that's just me. You can keep yours on if you want to. I'm not fussy.'

'Kate, I...'

'Oh come on, Rufus. You've just been ditched, and you were hardly in love with the poor cow. We used to be quite good together, I seem to remember. No harm in a friendly bonk for old times' sake, is there?'

Kate stood up briefly to kick off her shoes and wriggle out of her trousers and underwear. Rufus watched, open-mouthed, paralysed by a mixture of hopelessness and shock. Having removed all her own clothing, Kate began to pull at Rufus's t-shirt.

'At least take this off. Enter into the spirit of the thing. Don't worry,' she laughed, 'you haven't got anything I haven't seen before. I suppose most people say that when they get to the boxers.' She tugged the garment over his head and ran her hands down his arms, stroking his scars, old and new. 'There we are. All familiar chuffing ground to Yours Truly.' She unbuttoned his flies and wrenched his jeans down to his knees. Rufus remained inert, watching what she was doing with a bewildered detachment, still clutching his glass of wine, offering neither help nor resistance.

Kate straddled him once again, pausing in her diatribe to kiss him fiercely on his already smarting lip. She wriggled provocatively, running her hands over his chest and leaning down to suck his nipples in an attempt to arouse him. To Rufus's surprise, it worked.

Kate grinned.

'There you are! I knew you wanted to really. Hmmm, I remember you,' she said, slipping her hand inside his jeans.

She manoeuvred herself into position, lowering herself over him, and commenced energetic shagging. As she bounced away still she talked, on and on. Rufus was beyond passive, allowing her to do what she wanted, deriving little pleasure from the experience himself but completely unable to stop her.

Kate was enjoying herself. 'Ohh, that feels good. I really needed a fuck, I'm so horny these days. Mmm, I always did like your cock, you know. Always though it was one of the more cheerful things about you. Wow, you were so chuffing right about sex off medication. Who needs fucking pills when you can... mmmmm!' She speeded up, pogo-ing wildly, faster and faster, ever more excited. Rufus found himself barely stirred, his own breathing hardly altered.

'Yes!' Kate shouted. 'That's it! Oh yes! Fucking yes! Fuck me! Fuck me! Fuck you! Fuck fucking everyone!' She shrieked and screamed her way through a seismic orgasm.

Rufus had the curious impression that the squirrel was watching the whole sordid event and felt ridiculously embarrassed.

Kate slumped forwards on top of him, motionless and silent for the briefest of moments. Then, without even looking at him, she hopped from his lap. 'Christ, I needed that,' she said, grabbing his t-shirt and pulling it on over her head. 'Let's open another bottle of wine. Wait, I need a chuffing pee first.'

Rufus watched her disappear into the bathroom. He remained as he was, trousers down, boxers askew, cock shrivelling with shame. He gave a heavy sigh, a sigh that came from some other place. A place which recognised how very sad things were in the world of the New In-No-Way-Improved Rufus Waters. He still held his glass of wine. He regarded the gloomy red of the drink for a few seconds, aware of its bitter fumes above the sour scent of sex. He turned to meet the unwavering gaze of the disapproving squirrel.

'Bollocks,' he said, and drained his glass.

CHAPTER SEVENTEEN

When Kate woke up after her now customary four hours sleep she was briefly surprised to find herself in Rufus's bed. Her mind whirred into action, bringing back garish pictures from the day before. She studied Rufus sleeping beside her. He looked young when he was asleep, she decided. Well, younger, at least. Something about the way his face relaxed. No, not relaxed, it was just that he couldn't hang on to that so-chuffing-superior expression of his when he was sleeping. Huge bloody improvement. The doorbell interrupted her thoughts. She pulled Rufus's t-shirt on and, still knickerless, went to see who it was.

A clear-skinned blonde stood in the grey light of morning, her smile faltering at the sight of Kate.

'Oh,' she said.

'Hello,' Kate made no effort to rein in her natural cheerfulness, despite what could be seen as an Awkward Situation. 'You have got to be Abigail.'

'I was looking for Rufus.'

'That makes sense. This is his flat, after all. Good chance of finding him here.'

'Is he in?'

'He's asleep,' Kate lowered her voice to a conspiratorial whisper. 'Bit tired. We had a busy night. You know how it is? Of course you do, Rufus made a point of telling me how much he enjoyed shagging you.'

'What?'

'We're old friends,' Kate explained, not bothering to hold down Rufus's t-shirt as a naughty breeze lifted it to an immodest height. 'He tells me everything. You could say he's like a brother to me, but then that makes us shagging each other sound like incest, doesn't it?' she laughed. 'Whoops! Can't have people calling him a pervert as well as a nutter, now, can we? Do you want me to wake him up? I'm sure he'd love to see you.'

Abigail began to back away. 'No,' she said, 'it doesn't matter.'

'Don't be a silly beggar; you've come all this way. Daft not to see him. Least he can do is get his lazy carcass out of bed. Come on in, have some coffee. Rufus!' she yelled into the flat. 'Rufus! Wake up, Abigail's here.'

Abigail turned tearfully away and started down the iron staircase.

'Wait! Don't go. Rufus, hurry up. Dora the Explorer's leaving!'

Rufus appeared in the doorway, still buttoning his jeans. He called after Abigail.

'Wait, Abigail! Please don't go.' He hurried out onto the balcony in time to see her glance back at him, clearly upset and angry. His shoulders slumped, the fight gone out of him.

Kate came to stand beside him. 'Chuffing hell, Rufus, did you really fancy her? She's so...*healthy.*'

An hour later Kate had convinced Rufus that they should visit Teach. They battled their way through High Town against a tide of Saturday shoppers, Kate gesticulating and talking without pause. Rufus dived into an off licence for more wine. Ten more minutes saw them outside the shabby town house where Teach lived. The faded red brick was crumbling in places, and the windows sorely in need of repainting. What must once have been a grand family residence had long ago been turned into bedsits and was home to the collection of loners and losers.

Chuffing halfway house.

Kate frowned at the grubby, worn labels on the buzzers and leaned on the one left blank. As the intercom hissed into life she stepped forwards and yelled into it.

'Teach, you old bugger! Move your creaky bum and let us in. It's pissing down out here.'

The buzzer sounded and the front door clicked open.

Teach's room was up three flights of smelly stairs. He was waiting for them, still in his striped pyjamas.

'Fuck me, Teach!' said Kate. 'You look like you just stepped out of bloody Belsen. Could anyone actually get any thinner without chuffing disappearing? You look like death not even slightly warmed up.'

'Yes, sorry about that. Come in, my friends, come in.'

Kate paused on the threshold, pushing her face close to his. 'You want to be careful. There are some serious bugs around, you know. They travel half way round the world in chilled chicken wings just to get people like you.'

Teach smiled wanly. 'That'll be it then, I expect. Hi, Rufus. Find somewhere to rest your weary bones, people, please. *Mi casa, zoo casa,* and all that.'

Kate and Rufus squeezed their way into Teach's room. Despite having a high Victorian ceiling and an enormous window the space still felt cramped and claustrophobic due to the countless finds Teach had gathered. Somewhere under all the precious junk was ugly junk furniture – a sagging single bed, a stained sofa, a winged chair that had been diverted on its way to an old people's home, and a swirly-patterned carpet. The corner kitchen was made up of a dangerous cooker (short a couple of knobs), a sink that clearly was not chuffing stainless, a grubby fridge, a wonky cupboard, and a fold-away table that was folded away. Everywhere plastic bags sat fatly, their innards spilling out. At least they hid some of the revolting carpet.

Rufus held up the bottle of wine. 'Got a corkscrew?'

'Oh,' Teach brightened, 'a little early in the day, but why not? We all look in need of a small medicinal tincture.' He coughed loudly as if to underline the point. After a moment's noisy rooting he produced a corkscrew and handed it to Rufus. 'Glasses could present more of a problem, I fear. Still, seek and ye shall find.' He dug in a box behind the sofa. '*Et Voila!* Well, almost.' His search had yielded one pint glass, a china tea cup, and a chipped mug with kittens on it.

Rufus filled them with wine and sat at the window, staring blankly outwards. Teach lowered himself stiffly into the winged chair. Kate could not settle. Instead she wandered about, picking things up and putting them down again.

'How do you live with all this chuffing stuff, Teach? Haven't you ever got that spacey head of yours round the idea of spring cleaning?'

'Kate, my love, what you see before you is not, as you so charmingly put it, *stuff*. It is a collection of treasures, given up to me by the streets of our fair city. And, being a collection, by definition, it collects. *Ergo*, the available space is reduced over time. It is a price I am willing to pay.'

'It would drive me mad,' Kate said, and then laughed, 'not that anyone would notice the difference. Of course Rufus is anal about keeping his fabulous flat tidily untidy. He says he never cleans it but of course he bloody does. Real mess doesn't look like that. He's more house proud than my mam. Or at least, he is when he's not depressed. Which he is now. Give it a couple of weeks we'll have to send in the environmental health hit squad. Hah! Environmental! Definition of an area where nutters live!' She laughed again, loudly this time, a jagged edge to her cackle. She snatched up her mug of wine and slurped it carelessly, spilling some on Teach's bed as she passed. She spied his record collection and began flicking through. 'You are the only person I know who still has records. Let's have some music, liven things up a bit. Must be something bearable in here. Oh look, Simon and Garfunkel. Mam used to love them.' She slipped the record from its sleeve and plonked it on the dusty turntable. The needle dropped roughly onto the vinyl, causing Teach to wince.

'Whoops! Sorry,' said Kate, cranking up the volume. 'Here we go!'

The upbeat opening bars of *Cecelia* blasted into the room.

Teach coughed and nodded his approval, 'Oh, good choice.'

Kate grabbed Rufus's hand. 'Come on, let's dance!' she shouted above the rattling percussion.

Rufus scowled. 'Do I look like someone who wants to dance?'

'No, but it's you or Teach, and I might break him. Come on!' She dragged him to his feet, kicking aside a heap of bags to create a tiny space. Rufus attempted to tweak down the volume but Kate hauled him away from the player. With no regard for the smallness of the room, or anyone else's safety, Kate danced with bold expansive movements, letting the powerful beat of the music work with her frantic, wired mood.

Rufus stood and swayed feebly until Kate grabbed both his hands and began to move him, puppet-like, in a determined attempt to get him to dance properly.

Teach settled a little deeper into his chair, smiling and sipping wine from his bone china cup. 'Ahh, *otium cum dignitate*, one could say. Leisure with dignity.' His voice barely registered above the music, but that didn't stop him muttering on. 'It might interest you to know that Cecelia, about whom the boys are so ably singing, was, in point of fact, the patron saint of music.'

Kate and Rufus danced on. Teach rested his cup on the arm of his chair and closed his eyes. After a few seconds a frown clouded his face. Beads of sweat appeared on his brow. He coughed briefly. His body tensed and the tea cup jerked in his hand, sending up a small spurt of wine. His knuckles whitened, up a shade from alabaster to chalk. At once his eyes sprang open and an expression of mild surprise rearranged his face. He opened his mouth as if to speak but no words came. Slowly, his faced relaxed and his head flopped gently to one side. He sat, still as stone, his eyes open, the piece of Royal Doulton gripped in his hand. Kate and Rufus continued their disconnected dancing until the song came to an end. Only then did Kate sense that something was not quite right. She dropped Rufus's hands and stepped towards the winged chair.

'Teach?' for once her voice was soft. 'Are you OK? Teach?'

Simon and Garfunkel did not wait for a reply but threw themselves into the next number on the album. As their music filled the room Kate leaned forwards and touched Teach's cooling cheek and knew beyond the smallest chuffing doubt that he was dead.

CHAPTER EIGHTEEN

Rufus had reached the point in his depression he dreaded most. Sleeplessness. No matter what he did, how much exercise and fresh air he inflicted upon himself, how many soothing nightcaps, how many aromatherapy-laden baths, he could not sleep. His Prozac levels were being upped slowly but were as yet nowhere near sufficient in strength or regularity to be effective. His sleeping tablets had been cruelly rationed against suicide attempts, and tranquillisers were forbidden for the same reason. That insomnia was the most likely thing to compel him to try to take his own life seemed to be a factor no-one was willing to address. The upshot was that he now lay in his bed of stones, listening to the tinny ticking of his alarm clock as the small hours of the night crawled by. Again. There was something about the period of darkness between one and five that was terrifying. Anything earlier could, with some success, be passed off as evening, or a pleasurably late night. Anything after five, so long as you weren't in the very depths of winter, could be considered near-dawn. And near-dawn meant close to daylight. Close, indeed, to day. To Normal Waking Hours. When it was legitimate to be awake, whatever the crumbling state of your mind. To be awake (unwillingly awake) between the hours of one and five, however, was, officially, a Bad Thing. It meant you had lost control of yet another supposedly simple mental function - the ability to switch off and to drift away to that fluffy cloud of rest and temporary oblivion.

As far as Rufus could fathom, and he had had a lot of time to think about the matter, there were two crucial things about sleep. Things so fundamentally vital to anything remotely close to sanity that without them, you were a goner. The first of these was, simply put, the restorative power of sleep. The body needed to rest. The brain needed to rest. Both required several hours (female Prime Ministers notwithstanding) of undisturbed, comfortable slumber in which to heal and repair. Skin, for example. Skin did most of its getting better while a person slept. It was no surprise to Rufus that the scars on his arms remained red and raised for far longer than was normal. Nor that his broken finger continued to cause his GP to tut and shake his head long after it should have fused and mended and been useful once again. Of course, everybody knew about the effects on the mind and body of sleep deprivation. What loathsome torture. To so disorientate, so confuse, so addle, so drive to madness simply through preventing sleep. The sleep-starved victims stumbling and mumbling through each day, head full of cotton wool, eyes itchy and red, mouth dry, brain throbbing, limbs dragging, barely able to raise themselves under their own lethargic weight.

But for Rufus the other significant consequence of perpetual wakefulness was far more cruel. The absence of respite. The ceaseless continuation of his morbid state. For sleep was the only way to fully switch off the agony of his depression. Nothing else could quieten that evil creature that crouched inside him. Nothing else could ease the overwhelming sense of dread. Of impending doom. Of helplessness. Of sorrow. His stomach was filled with ice. His heart ached, as if some callous lover had broken it. And, after all, he was heartbroken: his love of life had left him, seemingly never to return.

And now there was Teach. Or rather, there wasn't Teach. Rufus opened his eyes and stared into the darkness of his bedroom. A vision of Teach's pale face drifted past. It was not an alarming sight. Teach had, when he thought about it, worn the look of somebody long deceased for years, and his face was unchanged by death. It could not get any paler. Still, there was a tragic poignancy about his friend's empty expression. Rufus blinked away the memory of that moment, but he could still hear Kate screaming.

He switched on the bedside light and squinted at the clock. Two forty-three. Should he get up? He decided he would. The wet autumn had chilled the flat, but he could not be bothered to turn on the heating. He briefly contemplated filling a hot water bottle, but the picture it presented of himself curled up around it was too pathetic to be seriously considered. He shuffled through to the kitchen and ignited the flame under the kettle. As he waited for it to boil he rooted through the cupboard in search of drinking chocolate. God, it had come to this. Cocoa! He was thirty-five, and he was alone, awake, miserable, and drinking cocoa. Like some aged, whiffy widower. Imagine, four more decades of this hell before he could, he reckoned, indulge in nocturnal hot chocolate without shame.

'Sod it' he said, and shook quantities of the dusty powder into the last clean mug. He added an equal heap of sugar. The fridge yielded a worryingly familiar carton of milk. He sniffed it. Borderline. He added it to the mug and stirred. He was still stirring when the kettle began to whistle, a comforting cloud of steam drifting about his head. He took his drink and went back to bed. Cupping the mug in his cold hands he waited for the contents to cool enough to be drinkable. After all, what was the rush? He had several hours to get through before morning. He blew on the cocoa then lost patience, sipped, and burnt his mouth. With a sigh he put the mug on his locker and switched off the light. The second he closed his eyes it all started again. Teach. Death. Life. That rat gnawing at his innards, chewing away hope and joy and love and all the things that made a person's existence tolerable.

He tried affirmations. One of the many ridiculous techniques one of the many ridiculous therapists had inflicted upon him. Positive thinking with a New Age twist. The idea that he was resorting to such a thing depressed him further, if that were possible. Still, what had he got to lose?

He cleared his throat. 'Peaceful sleep comes to me quickly and easily,' he said, self-consciously keeping his voice down. But why? Surely nutters were supposed to talk to themselves? It was expected of them. He tried again, a little louder this time. 'Peaceful sleep comes to me quickly and easily. I am safe and calm. I am safe and calm. Peaceful sleep comes to me quickly and easily.' He waited. Still nothing, not even the slightest hint of drowsiness. 'I said, "quickly and easily"!' he yelled into the gloom. Waste of sodding time. He reached over and switched on the radio. The World Service hissed into action. Bolivia, this time. Rufus was fast developing a good working knowledge of arcane customs and events going on in the more obscure corners of the planet. Why was there never a programme from somewhere he could actually point to on a map? And did anyone really care about the plight of the peasants whose livelihood depended on the longhaired capybara? He knew he didn't. No more than any of them cared about him. He would take up crossword puzzles. And then maybe there would be some point to all this ludicrous information he was filling his head with. But he knew it was no good resenting what was on offer. More than once it had been some far flung tradition or unfathomable piece of music that had rescued him from certain and irrevocable madness by sending him off to sleep. Only this time it wasn't working. He sat up and rolled his shoulders, turning his head slowly from side to side. His bones clicked and twanged alarmingly. He resisted the impulse to look at the clock again. No. That was always a bad idea and to be put off absolutely as long as possible. He wriggled down in the bed and forced himself to summon up something pleasurable in his head. A summer picnic. A beautiful day. Birds. Flowers. Food. Kate. Oh fuck, there was Teach again. Try something else. Quick, quick, before... no good. Too late. The Kraken in his belly had stirred. Rufus felt tears spring from his eyes. There was no point in attempting to stop them. Besides, why shouldn't he cry for Teach? Poor bugger. He would miss him. More than he wanted to think about. There were so few people in his life worth bothering with. More to the point, there were so few people in his life who thought he was worth bothering with. And Teach had been kind. And funny. And wise. And sufficiently bonkers to be comforting. Rufus sniffed and wiped his face with the back of his hand. He knew he was being pathetic and selfish, and he hated himself for it. For the truth was, however sorry he felt for Teach, he felt more sorry for himself. After all, Teach was out of it, home and dry. *He* was left behind to do the missing. To struggle on with life. Rufus became aware of a rushing noise in his ears. He'd heard it before. It was the part of him that might have made something of himself screaming out its loathing for the rest of him. And he did hate himself. He hated his self-obsession. He hated his lack of strength. He hated the way he hurt people who tried to love him. He hated the way that he was just a passive nothing, a person of no consequence who gave nothing. When he did, eventually, manage to die, who would care? The world would be no worse off without him in it. It might quite possibly be improved. There would be nothing left of him, nothing worthwhile. Just a few unflattering photos and an empty space at Matthew and Helen's table. His mother would be relieved, he was pretty sure of that. And Kate? Would she be OK? Who was he kidding? She wasn't OK now. What difference would it make if he weren't there? He wasn't in any fit state to help her. Not now, not ever.

He sat up and switched on the light again, glimpsing the clock face as he did so. Two fifty-nine. Two fucking fifty-nine! All that faffing about. All that exhausting effort expended trying to get to sleep had only used up sixteen sodding minutes. There had to be something else he could do. He slid open the drawer in his bedside locker and picked up a bottle of pills. He unscrewed the top and shook the contents into his palm. Four shiny red tablets. His ration until next Tuesday. Five days. That meant he was already ahead of his allocation and faced one night with no sleeping medication. But he could go back to Dr Spinks on Monday and beg. What a lovely thought. What a way to start his week. He would say Teach's death was making it even harder than usual for him to sleep. And it would be true. He watched as the pills rolled and glinted in his hand. Four. 50mg each. Not enough. Not nearly enough. With a sigh he tipped three of them back into the jar and twisted the lid back on. He popped the precious tablet into his mouth and looked for water in the glass by his clock. There was none. He snatched up his mug of cocoa instead and took a large swig of the tepid milkiness. He gagged and fought the urge to retch as the sour liquid washed the pill down his throat. Not borderline after all.

CHAPTER NINETEEN

St Dunston's church, a mile outside Hereford, was large
but dark. It had, in Kate's opinion, gone over the top with the
stained glass. All very well showing chuffing off, but how
was a person supposed to read a hymnbook? Even with her
mind skittering off in all directions she knew she was doing
a poor job of not letting herself think about never seeing
Teach again. The week following his death had been a blur
of ambulance, doctor, solicitor, funeral director, unknown
relations, and sobbing. She still couldn't believe he had gone.
One minute there they were, pratting about in his bedsit, him
rabbiting on in six buggering different languages as usual and
them dancing. Dancing! She glanced at Rufus sitting beside
her. He had been worse than useless. She hated him when he
was like this. She knew she shouldn't, knew she, of all people,
should be sympathetic and understanding. But she couldn't
be. Maybe it was because she knew, knew exactly what he
was going through. Maybe that was why she had no patience
with him. She never wanted to go there. Never wanted to
think about her own depressive state. Especially now, now
when she was high. Not that she would admit it, of course.
No way. She'd had every bugger telling her for the last month

she was going up. Had to spend her time denying it. It started with her GP, the bastard, whittering on about blood tests and lithium levels, then her CPN - *Just popping in for a little chat.* Chat my arse. You know you're in chuffing trouble when she starts sticking her nose in. Then it's Mam – *Are you alright, Our Katie? Have I to call Doctor Meadows?*

On and on they all went. Calm down, Kate. Take your medication, Kate. Don't get so wound up, Kate. Slow down, Kate. It was enough to drive any chuffer round the bed. Was it any wonder she ended up manic? Well, fuck 'em. Who were they to say what was best for her? How did they know what it felt like? Sad beggars. They were only half alive, most of them. They'd soon change their tune if they knew how she felt now. Why did they have to try and bring her down? What was so good about being down, for crying out loud? Look at Rufus. Did they really want her to be like him? To feel like that? No thank you. This songbird was flying and loving it. If the poor sad chuffers couldn't hack it that was their problem. She knew what she was doing. She was looking after herself. She was just chuffing fine, thank you all very much, and would everybody please leave her alone. Not so keen to tell her what to do when she was in a depression, were they? Oh no. Didn't see too many people flapping round Rufus right now. She looked at him again, her mouth hardening into a thin line at the very sight of his bowed head and deadened eyes. Thank fuck she wasn't like that now. Not now. Not with this to cope with. Poor Teach. Poor, lovely, sweet, gentle Teach. No beggar ever understood him either.

The church was surprisingly full. Who were all these people? Where had they come from? Where had they been when Teach was alive? They were mostly men and mostly dressed in smart wool coats or black Burberries. Nobody bought a black Burberry. Did they get them just for funerals? On the other side of Kate sat Teach's Aunt Beryl, a bird of a woman, couldn't be a day under eighty-five. Eyes like marbles underwater. Hankie pressed to her nose the whole time. At least they were real tears. She must have loved him. The coffin was only a few feet in front of them. Recycled cardboard. Trust Teach. A lovely touch. It looked like something he might have found out the back of the Chinese take away. The gerberas looked good on it, though. Excellent choice. No flowers! Fuck that. Had to have a bit of chuffing colour or they'd all go out and slit their wrists by the end of it.

Rufus's brother was taking the service. Kate liked him. She didn't go for priests on the whole, but he had a good heart. She could tell. Rufus sniffed loudly. Wasn't even up to dealing with his own chuffing snot. Kate pulled a tissue from her pocket and shoved it at him.

Matthew stepped up to the lectern and waited a moment for people to settle into silence. He smiled. 'Firstly, I would like to welcome you all here on behalf of Robert, or Teach, as I think most of us knew him.'

Kate couldn't help herself. 'Nobody called him chuffing Robert,' she said.

Matthew continued. 'It is heartening to see so many of you attending. I know it would have meant a great deal to Teach to see such a gathering of his former pupils and colleagues. He had such fond memories of his time as a Master at Whitecross.'

'It would have meant a deal more if they'd bothered with him while he was still warm,' Kate put in.

Matthew had clearly known mourners to sometimes let their anger get the better of them. He gave Kate a little nod and went on, 'To his friends, Teach's death was sudden and unexpected. However, it seems that Teach himself was aware of the seriousness of his condition, and of how advanced it was. He had gone to some trouble to make plans for this sad day. It was typical of him, I think you will agree, not to have complained about his lot, nor wanted a fuss to be made.'

Someone in a far pew blew their nose loudly.

'Teach,' Matthew explained, 'had very clear ideas about how he wanted this service to be. Ideas that may seem unorthodox, but perhaps no more so than the man himself.' He paused to look at the cardboard coffin. 'I am sure he would have appreciated the generous donations to the Belmont Hospital which have been made in lieu of flowers.' He turned and nodded at the verger, who was standing at the end of the choir stalls. There was a deal of fumbling. 'Teach asked that no words be said,' Matthew continued, 'nor lessons read. Instead he chose a piece of music that he would like you all to listen to. And I think he would have allowed that we remember him while we do so.'

There was a rumble from the speakers attached to four of the pillars. At last the music began. After a few stirring bars, Joe Cocker's gravelly voice picked up the Beatles' song.

'What would you do if I sang out of tune...'

In their seats at the front Aunt Beryl and Rufus wept silently. Kate gave way to sobbing noisily. Behind them some of the stuffier mourners looked nonplussed. Others smiled or even sniggered. Several throats were cleared as the music played on.

'Get by with a little help from my friends...'

As the short service came to an end people shuffled outside. The small car park behind the church was bumper to bumper with Mercedes and BMWs. By the lichgate stood Teach's hearse of choice – a white van, hired from a local self-drive firm. Rufus and three men from the funeral company made up the pallbearers. Teach couldn't have weighed more than your average anorexic by the end, and cardboard was so much lighter than chuffing oak. He wasn't a heavy load. Even so, with the man beside Rufus being a bit of a short-arse, the coffin had a daft tilt to it as it made its way down the tarmac path to the van. The gerberas dangled dangerously over one side. The back doors were opened and Teach in his packaging slid inside. Matthew got in behind the wheel, with Aunt Beryl and Kate up front, and Rufus and the pall bearers in the back. The drive to the Oaktrees Burial Ground was only three miles but took what seemed like forever. Matthew struggled to steer the van through the narrow lanes and crunched gears as he went, leaning on the horn on tight corners for fear of tractors. A slow snake of posh cars trailed behind them. The cemetery (for such it was, whatever alternative chuffing name they liked to give it) consisted of five acres of mixed woodland; a haven of tranquillity, and home to abundant wildlife, the sign on the gate said. By the time Teach was unloaded onto the ill-matched shoulders of the bearers for a second time the rain had started up again. Not gentle drizzle, or a light shower, or rain you could pretend wasn't happening and just get on with it. This was real rain. Rain that meant it. Heavy and hard and cold and driving down the back of your neck. The footpaths, already waterlogged after weeks of bad weather, could take no more. Puddles, which had covered most of the ground for days, were swelled in minutes to deep pools. The gritty paths quickly turned to slick, gloopy mud. The red, clay-rich Hereford soil sucked and pulled at polished leather as the mourners slithered their way through the woods. It was unfortunate that Teach's plot should be at the furthest possible point from the car park. Matthew's cassock trailed through the goo and was soon heavy with slime. People fought to keep umbrellas above their heads while grabbing at slender birches to steady themselves as they squelched deeper into the woodlands. Kate and Matthew took an arm apiece of Aunt Beryl, who was in danger of being lost in a flooded pothole in a second. Kate glanced behind her in time to see a chubby man with a military moustache fall flat on his arse. How could you not laugh at that? She caught a disapproving glare from a middle-aged couple and scowled back at them. Teach would have chuffing laughed. Kate stuck her nose in the air. Let the bastards wallow in the filth. They weren't worth the effort. Up ahead she noticed her flowers on the coffin had drooped beneath the weight of water and now floated in a deep puddle of their own. She could see now that the coffin itself was actually beginning to disintegrate. It had never been designed with such a deluge in mind, which was pretty short-sighted, when Kate thought of every funeral she had ever been to and seemed to recall rain. As she watched, the lid sagged and the edges and corners of the box became somehow blunted.

'Chuffing hell,' she muttered.

Matthew looked at her with eyebrows raised behind steamy glasses.

'The coffin,' she jerked her head, 'it's falling to bits.'

Matthew risked taking a hand off Aunt Beryl's arm to lift his specs for a better look.

'Oh, my word! Rufus!' he called ahead in a stage whisper. 'I'm so sorry, but I think we should proceed a little more swiftly,' he said.

Kate rolled her eyes, then yelled, 'Get a move on you lot, that crap buggering box'll be papier mache in a minute!'

The pallbearers stepped up their pace with difficulty. At one point their cargo lurched dangerously as the two men supporting the rear of the coffin lost their footing in the mud and slid sideways. They were saved by a stout ash tree, which bounced them back on course. The manoeuvre had the effect of forcing Teach's body forward in his flimsy casing, so that his feet began to kick their way through the end flap. By the time they arrived at the grave, Teach's scuffed brown brogues were clearly visible. For one awful moment it looked like the whole soggy mess of a coffin was going to give way and Teach would be putting in an unexpected appearance at his own graveside.

Matthew rattled his way through a shortened (and all the chuffing better for it) version of the burial service. Mud-splattered mourners gathered warily at the edge of the slippery hole. At last, with a deal of haste and very little in the way of dignity, Teach and his pathetic wrapping were lowered clumsily into the grave. The sight of the rain-filled, slimy gash in the earth that was to be Teach's resting place was too much for Kate to stand. Finally the whole absurd event had become unbearable. She turned her gaze from the muddy hole in the ground and rounded on the sodden group of anonymous mourners.

'What the fuck are you doing here? Why did you bother coming? Where were you when he was alive, you hypocritical, chuffing wankers? He loved your snotty fucking school. Fuck knows why. All he wanted was to be included. You were his family, for fuck's sake. You were all he had.'

Rufus stepped forward and took her arm. 'Come on, Kate,'

he said gently.

She wrenched her arm from him. 'No! These creeps need telling! You all think you're so bloody perfect. Here to pay your *respects*. Couldn't show the poor bastard any chuffing respect when you was alive, could you? No. And you know why not?'

Again Rufus tried to take her arm, to coax her away. Again she shook him off. 'I'll tell you why!' she shouted. 'Because you are all fucking cowards! You were scared. Every last one of you. Scared he might do something weird. Scared he might do something just a bit not nice, not normal. Scared he might embarrass you. You wouldn't show up until he was safely dead. The only good nutter's a dead nutter, isn't that right? You make me fucking sick, all of you!' She slumped to her knees in the mud, sobbing. Rufus crouched next to her, arms around her, letting her rock backwards and forwards against him as exhaustion overtook her. 'You make me sick,' she repeated, but her words were choked by tears and the relentless, heartless rain.

CHAPTER TWENTY

Lydia's house was as orderly and imposing inside as out. The Georgian drawing room was decorated in harmonious shades of mushroom and taupe, with sparkling white woodwork and flawless cornicing. It could never be misnamed a sitting room, or demoted to a living room, or, God forbid, a lounge. It was a drawing room. It was exactly as it should be, and people invited into it were expected to fit in quietly. Rufus hated the place and found himself longing for the clutter and chaos of his brother's house. He had allowed himself to be dragged to his mother's for dinner only because Matthew and Helen had picked him up. The fact that the meal was supposed to be by way of some sort of belated celebration of him getting a job didn't help. He hadn't yet told anyone there no longer was a job. God, it was going to be a long evening.

'Lovely and cosy in here, Lydia,' said Helen.

Matthew agreed, 'Just the place to be in this revolting weather. Do you want water in your Scotch, Rufus? Or have you seen enough of it lately?'

'Just ice, please.'

Lydia gave an impatient sigh. 'I'm surprised you're not all ill after getting soaked at that ridiculous funeral.'

'The rain kept you away did it, Mummy?' asked Rufus, taking a swift swig of his single malt.

'I only met the man twice. I know he was your friend, and I'm sorry he's dead, but I don't see the point in attending the funeral of someone I hardly knew.'

'Didn't stop you watching both your husbands planted.'

'Rufus...' Matthew gave him a pleading look.

'Sorry. It's been a difficult week.'

'Do you have any other kind?' Lydia asked.

Helen chipped in brightly, 'I must say I'm looking forward to supper. You always come up with something interesting, Lydia. What's in store for us tonight?'

'Beef Wellington.'

Rufus snorted into his glass. 'A bit of mad cow. How appropriate.'

Lydia glared at him. 'Are you planning to be snippy and unpleasant all evening, Rufus?'

'Of course he isn't,' said Matthew, topping up Rufus's glass and giving him a brotherly black look. 'Drink that and behave yourself. Mummy's gone to a lot of trouble to cook us a delicious meal.'

Lydia arranged herself elegantly on a button-backed chair. 'You can fix me one of those, too, Matthew. Dinner will be a little while yet.' She turned her attention back to Rufus, like a hyena circling to find a weak spot. 'So, tell us about your new job, Rufus. I find it quite hard to picture you actually in an office of some sort.'

'Spare yourself the effort – I quit.'

'What?' squawked Matthew.

'Already?' Lydia was incredulous. 'Had they even got your name on the door?'

'It wasn't that sort of job.'

Helen made placatory hand gestures, 'Never mind. All experience. You'll be better prepared for the next time.'

Lydia was unconvinced. 'Are you sure you weren't sacked?'

'Thank you, Mummy. I can rely on you to have faith in me.'

'I simply do not see why you would go to all the trouble of obtaining a position just to walk out after five minutes.'

'If you must know it was a mutual thing. They decided I wasn't right for the job about the same time I realised I couldn't do it.'

'But they'd only just given it to you. What did you do to change their minds so quickly?'

'I missed a couple of days, that's all. I was away on holiday and I broke my finger,' he waved his still bandaged hand at her pointedly, 'and, well, I just needed some more time off.'

'You never go on holiday. Who did you go with?'

'A friend.'

'A friend?'

'A girl.'

'A girlfriend?'

'Briefly. Not any more, so you don't have to worry about her either.'

'You've surpassed yourself, Rufus. You've managed to gain and lose both employment and girlfriend in the same few short weeks.'

Matthew came to stand between his mother and his brother, as if physically separating them could prevent further conflict. 'I think we should celebrate Rufus's progress. I really do. It was very well done, getting that job in the first place. And who knows, maybe things could be resurrected with the young lady?'

'Think I'll leave resurrections to your lot, thanks.'

Lydia was shaking her head, one Italian leather toe starting to tap with agitation. 'I knew it was too good to be true. All that talk of pulling yourself together and throwing away your pills. All just another childish, selfish bid to be the centre of attention.'

Rufus felt he was as close as he had ever been to hitting her. 'Do you really think I care about your opinion any more? You never believed I could do it in the first place, did you? Must have been hell for you, trying to decide which you wanted most – for me to be normal, or for you to be proved right and see me fail. Well, you can keep your sodding malt whisky and your beef bloody Wellington!' He spun on his heel and hurled his glass into the fireplace, where it exploded with impressive and satisfying force.

Matthew and Helen gasped. Rufus strode from the room, his brother's entreaties in his ears, his mother's voice saying, 'Let him go, Matthew. Just let him go.'

Outside the pavements were puddled and the gutters running with flood water. The saturated ground could finally take no more, and the rain of the past few weeks was beginning to back up in drains, to fill culverts and ditches, and, as still more water poured from the night sky, to overflow streams and rivers. Rufus cared not. He hurried to the end of the avenue and turned left, down towards the centre of town. All around, people were sandbagging their doors. He continued towards the river. He was about to make his way through Chipton Street when what he saw made him halt mid stride. A canoe. A red canoe was being paddled silently towards him. For an instant he feared he was experiencing some dreadful nightmare involving his disastrous trip to Wales. Now he could see, beneath the bilious illumination of the streetlights, that the roads were deeply flooded. Water lapped at the handles of abandoned cars. A policeman waded towards him.

'Sorry, sir. You can't go any further.'

'I live on the other side of the river. I want to get home.'

'Not this way. Not any way tonight, I'm afraid. The bridge is closed. The whole of the town centre is cut off, and the water's still rising. You'll need to find somewhere else to stay. Oy!' the policeman spotted a couple of youths attempting to push a car through the water. 'What do you two think you're doing?' He hurried off, setting up a wash that slapped against front doors as he passed.

Rufus watched him go. The idea of returning to his mother's house was unthinkable. Instead he turned down a side street, keeping the worst of the floods to his right, heading towards the river but further down town. The main bridge might be closed but no one would be watching the old footbridge. He hurried through the park and followed the river as close as he could get without having to wade. The faux gas lamps that lit the footpath at night were still working, and he could soon make out the narrow bridge. Although the park and the playing fields on the other side were under water the iron bridge itself traversed the river in a high arch, so that it was clear of the fast flowing Wye beneath it. Rufus paddled past the signs and the drooping tape that still insisted the bridge was Closed and Unsafe. He clambered over the barriers and started across. There were ominous creaking sounds. He clutched the railings, squinting into the gloom to choose the firmest, least slippery planks on which to walk. Out of the corner of his eye he was aware of the furious water below. The sight of it made him dizzy. He pressed on. As he reached the familiar midway point he noticed that the wood on which he was walking was not just slippery but actually rotten in places. He hesitated for a second, and in that moment there was an almighty crack, and the bridge broke in two.

Rufus felt himself dropping. Instinctively he clung on to the handrail, his damaged finger objecting painfully as any support under his feet disappeared, so that he found himself dangling above the wild water. The half of the bridge he had just crossed plunged into the dark foam and was swept away. Sounds of ancient ironwork coming under unreasonable strain filled his ears, even above the noise of the river. He struggled to hold on, knowing that he did not have the strength in his arms to stay as he was for more than a minute, before gravity would drag him down.

Then, to his surprise, he had the sensation that time was halted. As if he had unlimited hours to consider his situation and the best possible course of action. He looked down at the angry, swirling water. It would be so easy to simply let go, in every sense. All he had to do was give in, allow his fingers to uncurl, drop into the river, and very soon all his troubles would be at an end. No more sleeplessness. No more being tortured by his own ludicrous brain. No more icy dread in his stomach. No more pain tightening around his heart. No more suffocating sadness. No more disappointing people. No more plodding his useless way through life. No more life. He was aware of a familiar detachment, of the notion that he was watching what was happening to him from a distance. He recognised this feeling. After all, he had been here before. Not precisely here, of course, not dangling off a crumbling Victorian structure in the middle of a flood. But on the point of ending it all. Somehow though, this time was different. This time he hadn't chosen it. Hadn't munched his way determinedly through a month's supply of sleeping pills. Hadn't lain in a warm bath and opened the veins in his wrists. This time the path to oblivion had come his way by chance. A combination of family tensions, bad weather, and poorly maintained nineteenth century engineering. Was it that which made him pause? As if there were a proper way of killing oneself; an etiquette involved? No. It wasn't that. With growing astonishment, Rufus realised that he did not want to die. More than that, he actually wanted to live. The thought was so astounding, so unfamiliar, so utterly at odds with his state of mind, that it shocked him. Made him laugh out loud. Which in turn made him consider how absolutely raving he must look, swinging by his stringy arms above a watery death, chortling loudly. And yet, here was Sanity, an irresistible light in the darkness, beckoning, calling him back to safety, and to the world of the living and the normal. It would be nothing short of rude to ignore Her the first time She deigned to engage him in some sort of dialogue.

'Sod this!' he said to himself. With much undignified grunting he heaved himself upwards. Every pathetic muscle in his neglected body was strained to its limit. The effort was enormous. He gasped as he succeeded in hauling himself onto the sloping woodwork of the second half of the bridge. Then, just as he began to believe he might make it, the iron joists shuddered beneath him and slewed sideways under the force of the torrent. Rufus screamed, certain he was about to become entangled with rusting metal and worm-riddled planks and plummet into the river. He redoubled his efforts, cursing silently at his lapsed gym membership and his pointlessly broken finger. At last he landed, like an exhausted, over-sized trout, flapping wetly on the remaining part of the bridge. Further frightening sounds of disintegration spurred him on. He scrambled on all fours, feeling the bridge fall away from under him as he reached the safety of the waterlogged bank. He splashed on, not pausing until he was able to drag himself up onto a nearby park bench. When he dared look back it was to see nothing. Not a rivet nor a splinter remained of the bridge. Rufus slumped on the bench, eyes closed, his breathing beginning to steady, as the rain washed his face and trickled gently into his ears.

CHAPTER TWENTY-ONE

Kate sat at her makeshift desk and wrote her third letter of the day. She had already dashed off notes to both the County Council and the Environmental Health Department, informing them of her recent change of address. She had now officially taken up residence in her parents' garage. Of course, it was no bugger else's chuffing business, but Kate knew how these things worked. Bet your arse some nosey neighbour would be dobbing her in to the authorities, and before you could say Change of Use some suit from the Council would be round, blathering on about planning permission and health and safety. Get in first. Beat them at their own chuffing game. A letter meant she was doing things properly. A letter meant things were in writing. Meant they had to see she was serious and that she knew what she was about. Let them charge her chuffing Council Tax if they had to. Wouldn't stop her. And let them send who they liked to try and tell her it wasn't a proper place for her to live. How did they chuffing know? How could any bugger know better than Kate what she needed? She needed space. And she needed a safe place to be. A place where no-one could sneak up on her. No-one could spy on her. She didn't blame her parents, poor beggars, but really, any fool could see the security in their house was crap. Double glazing and a chuffing chain on the door! Who was that supposed to keep out? She had tried (God knows she had tried!) to get them to see how vulnerable they were, how they were leaving themselves open and unprotected, but they didn't get it. Wouldn't get it. Well, that was up to them. She had to take action. It had come to her the night after Teach's funeral. She had been having another shower, still trying to wash off the stink of that chuffing mud, and she had been singing. Why wouldn't she? Loads of chuffers sang in the bath and the shower. Harmless enough, you would have thought. But oh no, not on the poncy Whitefield's estate it wasn't. That skinny cow from across the road had complained. Not that she'd come herself. Too chuffing chicken. Sent her poor sap of a husband. Would she mind ever so not singing quite so loud in the middle of the night. Some people were trying to sleep, apparently. Well bully for chuffing them! Kate hadn't slept since Wednesday gone, but no beggar seemed to care about that. And it had only been one o'clock in the morning. So what if she wanted to shower more than other people? What right had they to tell her she had to stink? One or two of them were strangers to soap, if you asked her. Which no bugger ever did. So, there she was, having a shower, singing, in her own home, nothing illegal about that, was there? Noise pollution, he'd said. Noise fucking pollution? She wasn't playing chuffing reggae on a ghetto blaster. Wasn't banging out rave music in the garden on her Dad's car stereo. Wasn't waltzing drunk down the pavement yelling football anthems. Delibe's *Lakme* noise pollution? Bizet's *Carmen* noise pollution? Chuffing philistines. Her Dad had tried to keep everyone happy. *Maybe you could listen to music on your iPod instead, Our Katie.*

How was that the same as singing? She loved her Dad, but come fucking on. If a girl couldn't sing in her own home… well, things couldn't go on like that, could they? OK, if she'd had money she would have gone somewhere else, somewhere out of sight and ear-chuffing-shot of all those mean-minded buggers. But Quickshopper believed the minimum wage was there for a reason, and she was in no position to ask for a pay rise. Not just now. So, the garage it would have to be.

Of course her mam had started to whine on about the damp and no central heating. For chuff's sake! You'd think no bugger had lived before they discovered North Sea Gas. Her Dad had had a go too, blathering on about not wanting to keep the car in the driveway at that time of year. Like he cared more about his bloody Rover than he did about her. She hadn't even bothered to argue about that one. Just took the keys and moved the thing out, then locked the garage door.

She glanced up from her letter. She was, if she said it herself, pretty bloody pleased with the results. All that hard work had paid off. It was a bit bare, but she had everything she needed. She had dragged in the mattress off her bed and made a passable nest in one corner, with her CD player plugged in to the row of sockets on the extension lead. Next to that was her Dad's workbench, which she had adapted into a desk complete with angle-poise lamp and a good supply of paper and envelopes. She knew she would be needing those. And loads of pens, all different colours and thicknesses. Sod computers. If you wanted to express yourself properly you needed colour, and you needed a pen on a sheet of chuffing paper. Keep that connection. Keep it real. Keep it fucking real. On the other side of the desk she'd put up the folding table they used out in the garden for barbecues. She had a washing up bowl on that, and a demijohn of water, and a couple of buckets underneath. One for dirty washing water. One for using as a toilet. That one had a lid. Mam had tried to get her to promise not to use it, to come inside to the bathroom, but that was missing the point. Kate needed to be able to lock the door. Who knows how long she would have to up-drawbridge on occasions? She had to be properly prepared. Her mam had eventually seen she was serious and handed over a good supply of air freshener. The pink one was vile, but she didn't mind Autumn Sunshine. Mind you, now that she'd taken up fags again she pretty much couldn't smell any chuffing thing properly. Just Marlborough Reds. Delicious. Hit the spot every time. The floor she had mostly covered in rugs and mats taken from the airing cupboard, where her mam had an impressive stash of the things. The shaped ones for going round bogs and sinks she had arranged like a sort of jigsaw puzzle. She liked the effect. In fact, as soon as she had some spare time she planned to market the idea. Jigsaw Rugs. Fucking brilliant concept. She could see it in Marks and chuffing Spencer, selling millions. In the middle of the space was the metal dustbin her Dad used for burning garden clippings and stuff. Well, her mam did have a bit of a point about heating. Kate had hauled in a couple of bags of barbecue charcoal, some hedge cuttings, and an unwanted shelf unit to keep her going for now. And Dad had finally given in and let her take one of the armchairs from the front room. She'd played on his sympathies there, she felt a bit bad about that. Had told him she needed somewhere comfy to sit. Truth be told, it was the heaviest piece of furniture she could find. Let's see some clever bugger open the chuffing door with that in front of it! And then there was the shrine. That had taken her hours, but it had been worth it. She had chosen the bit of wall above the bed so everyone would see it when they came through the door. Just looking at Jamie Oliver's smiling face made her feel a bit calmer. Mam liked him too, and she'd had loads of magazines with his picture in. Kate liked the one of him cooking on the beach best. Of course, she was the first to see who he really was, to pick up the signs, to recognise what he was about. So chuffing obvious. How could no-one else see it? Loaves and fishes, for chuff's sake. She sighed and shook her head at the pitiful blindness of people.

Kate refocused on her letter. The green ink glowed on the page. She held it up to the light and read it through. It had to be right.

Dear Doctor Meadows, it ran. *First things first, I will not be able to make my appointment on Friday. I realise you are not going to like this, but let me put your mind at rest. Number one, I am not manic. I know Doctor Gregory has been speaking to you, whittering on about my lithium levels, shouldn't wonder. Well, stand down the chuffing cavalry. I am feeling very well. Better, in fact, than I have felt for ages. True, Teach's death hit me hard. But I am dealing with it. There is no need for more appointments right now. They serve no useful purpose and use up valuable resources which could be better spent on some bugger else. So, I will let you know when I need to come in for one of our lovely little chats, but don't go clearing dates in your chuffing diary for a while yet, OK?*

Number two, can you get this bloody CPN woman and her Home Treatment so-called Team off my back? Doctor Gregory is always banging on about keeping stress out of my life – well I find that lot seriously stressful. Coming round

*here with their sympathetic looks and soft chuffing voices. I
tell you, they'd drive anyone nuts, the way they probe and
prod and speak to you like you're bloody five years old.
I am a grown woman. I can look after myself. Please stop
them coming. They are no longer welcome, and will not be
admitted to my home.*

*Which brings me to number three (see how organised, and
calm, and orderly I am?). I am now residing in the garage
adjacent to my parents' house. I have their permission to do
this and the relevant authorities have been informed. Kindly
see to it that all future correspondence is addressed to The
Annexe, 16 Whitefield's Estate. I know you will be pleased to
hear of this step towards independence on my part.*

Now to numero quatro *(whoops, channelling Teach a bit
there!) - the real business of this letter – a subject close to
both our hearts (yes, I know you have one!) – that is, the
available treatment for those with bi-polar disorder. You see?
I* do *have an awareness and acceptance of my own condition,
whatever that fucking CPN bitch likes to say. Otherwise I
wouldn't be addressing the issue of treatment, now, would I?
Point is, I have long held that the received wisdom on the
matter is sadly lacking. Lacking in insight, and lacking in
being any buggering use. And as no other beggar seems to
give a shite about looking for a more reasonable and, chuff
it, more effective way of helping people, I've been applying
my own brain to the matter. I have recently spent some time
at the library – and the great and the good of the medical
research profession could do chuffing worse than read a
buggering book or two themselves. Any road, I have, to put
it bluntly, cracked it. Job done. Problem solved. Sorted. The
end. Goodbye, was all she wrote. So bloody simple, really,*

can't believe no bugger else has seen it before. And who do I have to thank for my enlightened state, I hear you ask? Georges Bataille. Georges Fucking I'm-a-Frog-but-never-mind Bataille! *Who knew? Get yourself a copy of* Eroticism *right now, Doc, and I promise you, all your problems are over. Well, all your patients' problems, but then, that's the same thing, isn't it? The man was a fucking genius. No, really. Sex and death. That's it. Simple as that. I'm telling you, that snail-sucker knew what he was on about. I'll try and make it simple, though obviously to fully understand the whole idea you'll have to read the chuffing book yourself – can't do all of your job for you now, can I? So, it basically goes like this – humans fuck to avoid death, it's the whole Eros and Thanatos thing (look it up, I don't have time to go into all that now). Sex and death. Death and sex. Can't separate 'em. Shouldn't try. But, and here's where it all goes badly chuffing pear-shaped, we are told from day one that we have to separate them. Aren't allowed to think of them together. No sir, no way. Only nutters and perverts do that. Sex linked with death? How disgusting! Immoral! Amoral, even! Well, hello! Wake up and smell the pheromones! It is the most natural, most chuffing* normal *thing in the world. And we are forbidden to even think about it. Ever. And what (and I ask this question of your profession as a whole, Doctor, so don't think I'm getting at you), what do shrinks and quacks chuffing expect will happen? OK, so the masses, the poor deluded, wheel-treading multitude, are too frightened and busy and worn out to stop and question, to stop and consider what they really actually need. Not what they want, 'cos that's a whole different bastard issue, but what they* need. *And what they* need *is to recognise and acknowledge and deal with their own real fucking impulses and drives, and not to have them fed to them in a neat little well-mannered nice-as-pie and acceptable form. The Victorians saw it, for Christ's sake. Look at their art. It's all pale-faced, dying, or sometimes even chuffing dead women, with buttoned-up men being all intense and restrained and in-sodding-control, while their women die and lie there, and they don't show any emotion, but all they want to do is shag the corpses and shag everyone else while the smell of death is still in their nostrils. Are you following this, Doctor? Please try and keep up. It's important, OK? It's about letting people be how they need to be. It's about* repression *and* oppression *and how they are so chuffing-absolutely-linked to* depression, *and why can't anyone else see it!? Don't you* see *it? Madness is a perfectly sane response to how we are expected to live. Half the chuffing inmates at the Belmont are suffering societal induced lunacy. Chemical imbalance my arse! You get labelled depressive, schizoid, bi-polar, what-chuffing-ever, and then everyone watches you whiz about on your Loony-cycle, nodding their overpaid heads. See, they cry, we were right, she's nuts! They are all nuts! Well, who fucking drove us nuts, have you thought of that, you useless bastards?*

Kate was just warming to her subject when she heard a gentle knock on the door connecting the garage to the house. Her mother appeared carrying a plate of sandwiches.

'Thought you might like a bite to eat, Our Katie.' She hesitated on the threshold, holding out the food as if offering it to a dangerous animal.

'Ta, Mam, stick it down somewhere, will you? I'm in the middle of a letter.'

'Who are you writing to?'

'Doctor Meadows. For now. Although this needs to go further, to be chuffing honest. Its scope is well beyond his reach.'

The doorbell rang, and Kate's mam turned to go and answer it.

'Wait! Don't open that door.' Kate sprang to her feet and darted over to the window. She tweaked aside the blanket she had hung up as a curtain and peered outside. 'Chuffing knew it! It's that bitch of a CPN. And she's got a Social Worker with her.'

'The nurse with the red hair? Ooh, I thought she were lovely.'

'You would, Mam. No offence, but you don't know what we're dealing with here. She's poison, I'm telling you. Want an example of power corrupting? Take a look at a low ranking mental health worker. It's all there, in their eyes. Control freaks, every last one of 'em. It's what attracts them to the chuffing job.' She saw her mam's puzzled expression. 'She's not a nice person, Mam. Tina the Tyrant! OK?' she sighed and shook her head. 'Never mind, I wouldn't expect you to get it. Look, tell them I'm sleeping. No, no, wait. They'll just hang around drinking you out of Typhoo. Tell them… oh, fuck it. No, let 'em in. I'll talk to them. Show them I'm lovely and calm and very happy, ta very much. Yes, let them in.'

'In here?'

'Yes, in here! Of course, in here. *In here* is where I live, isn't it?'

Her mother hurried to the front door. Kate straightened herself up on her kitchen chair and squared her shoulders.

The Community Psychiatric Nurse was called Yolanda. Kate thought this was an unhelpful name. She might have got away with it in a big fat cosmopolitan city somewhere, but for the provinces, it was a deal too exotic and not a bit convincing. As if she were working under an assumed name. And for good chuffing reasons. Kate reckoned she must be on a long list of people who would quite like to do the woman harm if she thought she could get away with it. The Social Worker was a new face. She smiled a lot and said hello and how much she liked the room. Kate decided straight away that she wasn't worth bothering with and so ignored her.

She gestured for them to sit on the pile of bedding while her mam went off to make tea. The two women struggled to arrange themselves on the muddle of duvet and cushions. Kate held her position on her chair, enjoying looking down on the others.

'So,' Yolanda took in her surroundings as she spoke, her eyes lingering on the picture of Jamie Oliver's head stuck onto a muscular, nude male body, 'I see you've made yourself very comfortable in here, Katherine.'

Katherine! No bugger called her Katherine. Couldn't the stupid woman be arsed to find that out at least? It was insulting. Bitch.

'It'll do me,' Kate said. 'I don't need anything posh. Nothing pretentious. Just simple, and safe. Somewhere I can be left alone.'

'And how are you feeling today. In yourself?'

Kate wondered what that was supposed to mean? In yourself? Stupid bitch.

'Fine, ta. Just fine. No problems.'

'That's good. And have you taken your medication today?'

Like I'd tell you if I hadn't! And we both know it. Patronising bitch.

'First thing this morning,' Kate assured her.

Yolanda checked her notes. 'I see you've an appointment with Doctor Meadows for the day after tomorrow. You are going to attend, aren't you, Katherine?'

Ooh, that was plain chuffing nasty! No more room for wriggling. No more games. Clever Bitch.

'As it happens, I was in the middle of writing a letter to Doctor Meadows when you lot interrupted me.' Kate waved the pages of lined paper and green scrawl at them. 'I have explained why I won't be attending this time. The reasons are all in here.'

'And they are…?'

Don't push your luck, Bitch.

'Private,' Kate told her, setting her teeth. She noticed Social Worker rub her hands together. She leapt to her feet. 'Are you cold? Can't have that, can we? Not to worry, I've thought of everything in here. See? This place's even got its own central heating.' She swept her hand in the direction of the tin dustbin, then started stuffing in bunched up newspapers and handfuls of twigs. 'Soon have you warm as toast. Then you can report back to the good doctor that I am happy and well, and nice and calm, and looking after myself properly.'

Kate struck a match and lobbed it in with the sticks. It went out. She tried another, but the same thing happened.

'Shite!' she said, and poked at the newspaper with a stick. 'Chuffing light, will you.'

Yolanda stood up. 'Perhaps it would be better if you left that, Katherine? I'm not sure it's very safe to light it in here.'

'Safe? Of course it's safe. Ah, there we go.' She stepped back as flames shot up from the bin. The wet wood crackled and spat. She heaved the bag of charcoal across the floor, lifted it up, and tipped most of it in. The flames subsided.

The Social Worker was edging towards the door. Yolanda put a hand on Kate's arm.

'I really do think you should leave that now, Katherine,' she said.

Kate ignored her. Smoke began to billow up, quickly reaching the low ceiling. She laughed as more crackling and spitting heralded a whoomph of flames.

'There she blows! Look at that. Fucking brilliant. We should get some sausages, have a barbecue. Where the fuck are you going now?'

The two women scurried out of the room, just as Rufus entered it. He sprinted over to the workbench and grabbed the demijohn of water. He manhandled it across the room to the burning brazier, and emptied the contents over the flames. There was a deal of hissing and then a strong smell of damp charcoal.

'What the fuck did you do that for?' Kate screamed at him, not bothering to move as gritty water washed out of the bottom of the dustbin and soaked her feet.

'Kate, you can't have a fire like that inside. Look at the smoke,' Rufus took down the blanket and opened the window.

'It'll settle down in a minute. Chuffing hell, why does every bugger have to panic? Am I the only one who can be a bit calm around here? Talk about bloody overreacting. What are you doing here, anyway?'

'Your mother phoned me.'

'Well your timing was fab – you saw off that bitch and her chuffing useless sidekick. Don't think they'll be back in a hurry.'

'Kate, I…'

'What?'

She stood, hands on hips, head on one side, smoke swirling about her head, feet in a black puddle of water, and waited for him to explain himself.

Rufus gave her a rueful smile. 'Why don't you eat your sandwiches?' he said.

The two of them sat on the workbench, the bedding area being too wet to use now, and he watched as Kate chomped away at her lunch, talking all the while.

'Aren't you going to have one? They're chuffing good. Mam knows how to make a sarnie, I'll give her that. Here, have a look at this. My letter to Doctor Meadows. No, wait, I'll read it to you.'

And so she did. And the letter she had written to the Council. And the one to Environmental Health. And then she spent a busy hour putting forward her theory of Jamie Oliver being Christ, and how chuffing obvious it was, and how things were going to change big time now he was around again. She had just got to the part of her theory that explained how Jamie was going to bring the satanic supermarkets to their knees when a police car drew up outside. And an ambulance. Kate spotted them at once.

'Fucking bastards!' she shouted, spitting white sliced everywhere. 'Quick, Rufus, help me with this!' She pushed at the armchair, struggling to slide it in front of the door.

'Kate…'

'Don't just sit there, you lazy chuffing beggar, give us a hand! They think I'll let them drag me off again. Well I'm ready for the fuckers!' She grunted as the chair bumped into place up against the door. 'Come on, you bastards!' She screamed, 'I'm ready for you!'

She stood back.

Voices could be heard inside the house. Her Mam. The social worker. A doctor. Two coppers.

There was a gentle tapping.

'Our Katie?' her mam's voice had a wobble in it. 'Can you come out, love? The doctor is here to see you.'

'I'm not budging! Get yourself upstairs, Mam, out the way. If they want me they'll have to fucking come and get me. Just let them try!'

There was a bristling silence. Kate held her breath, fists clenched, waiting for the pounding and the battering to begin. Then, with the faintest of clicks, the handle turned and very slowly the door opened. Outwards. A willowy policeman appeared behind the armchair.

'Let's just move this to one side, shall we?' he said gently, and proceeded to push the chair out of the way.

Kate stayed frozen to the spot for a moment, thrown by this unexpected turn of events, and then she snapped. Screaming like a banshee she made a dash for the window. The doctor caught up with her.

'Now then, Kate,' he said, putting an arm out to her as she clambered onto the workbench to get to the open part of the window, 'come down from there, please. We don't want you hurting yourself.'

'Get away from me, you bastards, get away! Leave me alone!' She kicked out behind her, her foot connecting with the doctor's jaw and sending him sprawling onto the grimy wet floor. Suddenly the room was full of people. In her desperation to get out Kate broke the window. Shards of glass sliced into her hand and blood splattered the walls as she fought off the two policemen. 'Get off me! Rufus! Rufus, help me! Don't let them take me. Stop them, Rufus, for fuck's sake, stop them!' she bellowed. But he hung back, slipping away from her, until he was lost behind them, behind all those chuffing bastards who wanted to drag her away, to lock her up, to make a prisoner of her. 'No!' she screamed. 'No!'

But the tall copper had her hands pinned behind her back. The second one helped the social worker wrap a bandage around her bleeding palm. The doctor drew a syringe from his bag. Kate writhed and struggled with all her strength, causing her assailants to drop with her to the floor, where one of the policemen knelt on her. She opened her mouth to scream again as the needle plunged into her arm. She felt her heart labouring, her breath slowing, her mind blurring at the edges. She summoned a voice that was so faint and flimsy it seemed to come from someone else, someone a long, long way away.

'Rufus… Rufus *please!*' she whispered, before falling into oblivion.

CHAPTER TWENTY-TWO

Someone had spent a deal of money on landscaping the gardens to the front of the Belmont Hospital in an effort to stop the place looking as grim and frightening as it otherwise might. They need not have bothered. No amount of red-leaved vines, drooping wisteria, or Japanese maples could disguise the forbidding nature of the building. It always had been, and would always be, an unhappy mix of blue-grey stone and rusty-red brick, its Victorian origins unmistakeable, its institutional purpose brutally plain, no matter how many blooms dangled, like tired Christmas decorations, across its lumpen portals. Rufus quelled a shudder as he went inside. His own experiences of the place were too numerous, too painful, and too likely to be added to in the future for him to be able to put them to one side. The walls, with a complete lack of imagination or insight, had been painted institutional magnolia. The floor was covered in cracked, black and white vinyl. The hall was now the waiting room, and home to a mismatched assortment of uncomfortable chairs, wood-effect low tables, and a corner full of chewed toys. A scruffy heap of uninteresting magazines lay ignored on one of the tables. Half a dozen people sat in limp silence.

Whether visitor or inmate, it was not a building he wished to linger in one oppressive moment longer than was necessary. He made his way to the reception booth as quickly as his shaky legs would allow. A shockproof nurse sat on the other side of shockproof glass.

'I'm here to see Kate Browning,' Rufus said. 'She was admitted last night.'

'Are you a relative?'

'A friend. A close friend.'

The nurse checked information on the computer in front of her.

'Yes, she is here,' she said, 'but I'm afraid you can't see her at the moment.'

'Please.'

'Her parents are with her, and Doctor hasn't finished his rounds yet. Perhaps you could come back later. Or tomorrow.'

A soft voice behind Rufus made him turn. Kate's father, pale and plump, walked towards him.

'Hello, Rufus. I thought I saw you come in.' He offered a strong, broad hand.

Rufus shook it feebly. 'I'm so sorry about Kate,' he said. 'How is she?'

'Aye, well, you know how it is.' For a moment it looked as if the older man might start to cry, but he rallied. 'But, she's in the right place now. Her mam is with her. We're just waiting for Doctor Meadows.'

'I'm sorry,' Rufus said again. What else was there to say? As always, he felt he had let her down. Felt he should somehow have been able to help her, to stop it getting to this God-awful point. Did it have to end like this every time? Was there no sodding way of avoiding it?

As if reading his mind Mr Browning said, 'There really was nowt you could have done. Nowt any of us could have done. She'd not been well these past few weeks, you know, what with pressure of the Concert an' all. And then poor old Teach dying the way he did. So unexpected. Such a shock for our little Katie.'

The two men stood together for a moment in shared torment, driven to despair by their own helplessness. At last Kate's dad tried a smile.

'Would you like to see her, then? I'm sure it'd cheer her up.'

Rufus stifled a laugh. After all the years Mr Browning must have watched his cherished daughter losing the plot, after the kilos of pills, the weeks of incarceration, the months of therapy. After the shattered dreams and the lives of turmoil and anxiety they were forced to live. After all that, still the man believed that a friendly face could cheer poor, dear, mad Kate up.

'They won't let me,' Rufus told him, nodding his head at the now gum-chewing nurse.

'Oh, I'm sure it'd be alright.' Mr Browning leaned nearer the glass and spoke as if to one of the inmates. 'He can come through, can't 'e lass? Just for a mo?'

The nurse gave a reluctant roll of her eyes. 'Ten minutes,' she said, 'not a second longer.'

In the side room flimsy curtains with an inappropriately cheerful pattern hung limply at the windows. Two metal lockers leaned against one another in the corner. There were three beds. Two were empty. Kate lay on the third, propped up against an abundance of pillows, her feet curled beneath her under the thin sheet. Rufus's heart constricted at the sight of her. She looked so very tiny and so very frail. Her mother sat on the plastic chair beside the bed. Kate did not stir as they entered the room. Her eyes were closed, but somehow Rufus sensed she was not asleep. Mrs Browning smiled bravely at him.

Kate's dad leaned over the bed. 'Hey up, Our Katie, look who I found.'

Mrs Browning squeezed Kate's hand. 'Rufus is here. 'E's come to see you,' she said.

Rufus stood awkwardly at the foot of the bed. Kate remained inert and unresponsive. Mr Browning gently took his wife's arm.

'Let's go and get a cup of tea, shall we? These young people don't want us old fogies about, now, do they?'

'Please,' Rufus protested, 'don't leave on my account.'

Mr Browning shook his head. 'That's quite all right, Rufus. Tell the truth I could murder a cuppa. We'll see y'later. Come on, Mam,' he said, leading Kate's mother from the room. As he was on the point of leaving he hesitated. 'Don't expect too much from her at the moment,' he said. 'You know how it is, at this stage. We none of us like seeing Our Katie like this,' emotion began to choke his voice, 'but it's for the best. For now.' He mustered an unconvincing smile. 'Doctor Meadows said last night he'd be recommending another course of ECT. That seemed to help last time, didn't it?'

After they had gone, closing the door noiselessly behind them, Rufus went to stand by the bed. Kate's eyes were still closed though he still could not be sure she was sleeping.

'Kate?' he said softly. When she did not respond he tried again. 'Kate?' He leaned forwards and took her hand in his.

At last she opened her eyes and slowly, oh so slowly,

raised her head a little. She frowned, as if struggling to focus, battling to recognise the person before her. Gradually, with leaden speed, a lopsided smile rearranged her features.

'Rufus,' her voice was a hoarse whisper, her words slurred as if her tongue were too fat for her mouth. 'Rufus.'

He sat down on the edge of the bed.

'Hello,' he said.

'What are you doing here?'

'I came to see you.'

'Did you? How sweet.'

They sat in silence for a while, Kate's eyelids fluttering from time to time. With the back of her hand she wiped dribble from the side of her mouth. Rufus plucked a tissue from the box on her locker and handed it to her. She took it in fumbling fingers and smiled at him again.

Inside Rufus, a battle was raging. A battle between fury and sorrow. Fury at the unfairness of life that inflicted such horrendousness on such a wonderful human being. Sorrow at seeing the person he cared most for in all the world so beaten, so deadened, so crushed, by her own psyche and by what passed for treatment. He bit his lip to stop himself crying. If he started to weep now he knew he would not stop.

'It stinks,' he said through gritted teeth. 'This illness of yours. It stinks.'

Kate shook her head slowly, her dark curls dragging across the pillow. 'What would I be without it, Ruf? It *is* me, don't you know that, you daft beggar?' She dabbed at her mouth with a shaking hand and went on, 'It's my Siamese twin. I'd die if they took it away.'

'I hate it.'

'Then you hate me.'

'No I don't. I love you.'

'You can't just love bits of a person.'

'It's not fair.'

'Now you sound like a little boy.'

'You don't deserve this.'

'Nobody does. That's not the point.'

'We are so fucked.'

'No.'

'Yes. I can't help you. There's nothing we can do for each other. I just have to watch it happen.'

'Well, you know how I love to have an audience.'

'It's not funny.'

'No.'

'Marry me.'

'Hah! Now that *is* funny.'

'I mean it, I'm serious.'

'Chuffing hell, Rufus. Can you imagine? Mr and Mrs Lithium-Prozac! Right pair we'd make.'

'What else is there? What else can I do?'

'As my dad would say, *nowt*.' Rufus let go her hand but Kate reached over and took his, squeezing it with effort. 'You're here,' she said shakily. 'That's what counts. You're here.'

He looked at her, his eyes brimming.

'I do love you,' he said. 'Every last barking mad, sodding bit of you.'

Kate nodded. She turned her head as a slender shaft of sunlight fought its way through the grubby window.

'Look,' she said, 'it's stopped raining.'

Rufus screwed up his eyes to focus through the glass at the clearing sky outside. He raised her hand to his lips and kissed her fingers. 'Yes,' he said, 'it has.'

* * * * * *

Rufus held tightly onto Kate's hand. The metal of the park bench on which they were seated felt warm through his shirt. A heatwave in March was not unheard of, but it was pretty darn rare in Hereford. He stretched out his legs, leaning back to luxuriate in the sunshine. The park was alive with colour. Spring bulbs nodded their heads happily in the gentle breeze. Children ran about and played in summer clothes. Trees blossomed. It was as if the whole world had thrown off its winter wear once and for all, and a brighter, sunnier planet had emerged. Rufus regarded Kate fondly, smiling at her.

'It's good to see you well again,' he told her. 'I've missed you. I always do.'

'All part of my master plan – keep getting myself thrown in the Bin so that you'll pine and realise how much you care.'

'It's an original technique.'

'Works every chuffing time. Besides, I always come out looking my best. Think it's them plugging me into the National Grid. Gives a girl a certain glow. And does wonders for the hair. Bet you always thought these curls were natural.'

'Maybe I should try it.'

'Nah, you might lose that moody, melancholy thing you do so well. I could go off you completely.'

Rufus smiled and turned to gaze at the river. The gentle, calm, silky river that seemed to be a very distant relation to the surging torrent of the previous year. A pair of swans glided by. Rufus sighed, a good sigh. A happy letting go of so much that he knew he should long ago have rid himself of.

'You know,' he said, 'I don't think I'll bother trying to be sane after all.'

'Glad to hear it. I could never be friends with someone less chuffing screwed up than me.' She grinned at him. 'Is that a good enough reason to stay barking?'

He nodded, 'Good enough for me.' He held her gaze for a moment and then sprang to his feet. 'Come on, you'll be late. To the workhouse!' He squeezed her hand and swung her arm as they walked briskly through the park towards the town centre.

'I suppose you're going to loaf about all afternoon as usual,' said Kate.

'It is what I do best. I'll leave Rice Krispie control to you. You're the expert,' he told her.

'Chuffing right I am,' said Kate, stepping around a one-legged pigeon on the footpath. 'Chuffing right.'

the end

About the Author

P.J. Davy has considerable first- and second-hand experience of mental health issues, and these informed the writing of this book. However, the views expressed by the characters are not necessarily the views of the author.

P.J. Davy has an MA in Creative Writing from Lancaster University and regularly runs classes and workshops, where she finds, thanks to her students, that she learns every bit as much as she teaches. She lives in a remote part of Wales, which limits distractions to sheep and buzzards, neither of which she has so far been able to engage in time-wasting conversation, despite repeated attempts. She writes for several hours at a stretch, stopping at the witching hour of 3.30pm, after which time her small children demand she turn back into a mum. There is nothing like strong tea and three games of Spongebob Ludo to keep a person grounded.

The author also writes historical fantasies under the name Paula Brackston.

A Reading Guide for Book Groups

How 'Nutters' Was Written

Writing a comic novel about a serious subject has been a curiously liberating experience (and one I aim to repeat). The very human and intensely personal issues surrounding mental health problems are dear to my heart, and I would never want to sound flippant about them, nor to trivialise anyone's pain. Rather, what I aimed to do here was to produce a piece of writing that was entertaining and accessible, whilst also being thought-provoking and instructive. Looks remarkably simple, written down in a single sentence like that. Of course, it proved to be nothing of the kind. How far could one explore the dark side of a character's psyche without losing the comic tone of the book? How much should (could?) that comic style be sacrificed or compromised to honestly portray the suffering and despair endured by someone with, for example, depression? It was a challenging combination, and the chances of getting it horribly wrong were very real.

So what's liberating about that, I hear you cry? In a word, honesty. I found that the only way to express the story in the style and tone I was striving for, while also being true to the subject matter, was to be totally honest. On both counts. Honest in writing of the pain and difficulties faced by a startlingly large proportion of the population at some point in their lives. And honest in the way in which I felt the story could best be told. And, to be honest, for all the bleakness and sadness involved in mental illness, a great deal of it is unavoidably funny. Once I allowed myself to simply not hold back, to just to say it how it is, or at least, how I think it is, then 'Nutters' pretty much wrote itself. And after all, isn't truth what writing is all about?

Points for Discussion

• Did you feel comfortable reading a comic novel that explored aspects of mental health problems? What are the advantages and disadvantages of using such a writing style to tackle this subject?

• It was important to me that the self-harming character be a man - I believe a woman (and her illness) would have been perceived quite differently. What do you think?

• Who did you find you had more sympathy for, Rufus or Kate? Why?

•   How do you think the question of medication was tackled in the story?

•   Rufus makes the point (to Kate, in chapter 3) that his privileged background often worked against him because people thought he had no reason to be depressed. Do you think he has a valid point? How does this prejudice influence his decision to sack his psychiatrist and stop taking his medication?

•   Teach is very important to both Rufus and Kate. What impact did his death have upon them?

•   'Nutters' is very much concerned with what it means for people to be true to themselves. Who is most successful at this, Rufus, Kate, or Teach?

Mind is the leading mental health charity in England and Wales.

For details of your nearest local Mind association and of local services, contact the Mind*info*Line on 0845 7660 163 Monday to Friday 9.00am to 5.00pm or visit www.mind.org.uk